CAGED MOON

FATED MATES BOOK 6

KITTY THOMAS
ZOE WINTERS

CAGED MOON

KITTY THOMAS
ZOE WINTERS

FATED MATES BOOK SIX

INCU BOOKS

Caged Moon (Fated Mates, Book 6)

(c) 2014 Zoe Winters, (c) 2021 Zoe Winters, Kitty Thomas

Printed in the United States of America

ISBN-13: 978-1-938639-81-4

Wholesale orders can be placed through Ingram.

Published by IncuBooks, an imprint of Blue Pencil Media

Contact: kittythomas29@gmail.com

For Lesley P.
Here, have some more werewolves. :)

1

2 *6 years in the future.*

THE REINFORCED steel made an ominous sound as Sydney slammed the door. Her room was windowless, but that might be because it was underground. Not much of a view except for the earthworms. A moment later the door opened again, and her father—the vampire king— stood framed in the doorway, eyes glowing in what she was sure he felt was an ominous threat. She'd seen it so many times the effect had blunted.

She was too old for this fight. Instinctively she knew it. She'd become emotionally-stunted at adolescence, but he would never set her free. How could she discover who she was or how to be anything other than a child if she never left home?

"Dad! I'm twenty-seven. You can't keep me locked away in your creepy compound for the rest of my life. However long that turns out to be!"

She might be immortal or she might have a normal human lifespan. They didn't know. She was an oddity in the vampire world: born, not made. Her mother was human and the vampire king's claimed mate. The claiming was the thing that made Sydney's bizarre existence possible. She wished her parents had thought to use birth control because she had all the weaknesses of a vampire and none of the strengths.

Anthony growled. "I am trying to *protect* you. It's not safe out there! You know it's not safe."

"Just get OUT! And send Jacob in. I'm hungry."

The blond vampire's hands clenched and unclenched at his sides as if he wanted to throttle her but feared he'd kill her if he ever gave in to temptation. "I don't like you alone with him. He could hurt you."

They'd had this conversation for nearly ten years now. Yet another stale script.

Sydney rolled her eyes. "Then maybe you should have let *me* claim him instead of one of your minions."

"I won't allow my daughter to be mated to something so pathetic. He couldn't protect you from a horsefly let alone a genuine threat!"

It wasn't as if the vampire suitors were lined up down the streets. She'd never find a mate locked up here, that was for sure. And living here forever with her parents was just too humiliating. Practically every vampire left standing after the war wanted her dead because she was so weak. And they didn't like for weak things to live.

Anthony disappeared down the hall and returned minutes later with Jacob in tow.

The human was Sydney's age, one of many boys brought in for her to feed from over the years—just another thing that made her entire existence ghoulish. A five-year-old girl sucking the blood from a similarly innocent boy's throat was disturbing in the extreme. She was glad she could barely remember it. She'd blocked out many of those she'd accidentally killed over the years.

Since the preternaturals lost the war and humans were protected in their magically warded cities, stray humans had become harder and harder to come by. It was necessary now to secure a permanent food source and lock it in through a mating. There was no more free range feeding unless it was wildlife in the forest, and that could only take you so far.

When Sydney was seventeen, it was decided that she should have a single, safe food source who wouldn't die from too much blood loss.

Elise, a vampiress in the king's employ had been ordered to claim Jacob as a mate and allow Sydney to feed from him. It was a mating of convenience—or by royal decree. Elise, not wanting to lose her safe resting place inside the vampire compound, had reluctantly and bitterly agreed, knowing she could never claim nor be claimed by another if she ever found real love.

The bitch hated Sydney for it, and the feeling was mutual. If Anthony was so concerned for her safety, maybe he should get rid of Elise instead of worrying so much about the human.

"Well," Sydney said, "are you going to just stand there and watch? Can I just say, gross?" While it hadn't been that way in the beginning, once she'd become a teen, her feelings about feeding had shifted. It had become something her parents were not welcome to observe. She needed privacy. "Go!"

"If you hurt her..." Anthony growled at the human.

"I'd *never* hurt her," the man said.

Sydney thought Jacob was half in love with her. He was a good-looking man, but the feeling wasn't reciprocated on her part. Even if it had been, it would be too weird that he was another vampire's mate, even if in name and mystical link only. Sydney couldn't let herself get attached.

"Dad, get out. I swear to you I will intentionally starve to death if you keep standing there."

Anthony's eyes flashed red, but he grumbled something incoherent and left, shutting the door behind him.

When she and Jacob were alone, Sydney deadbolted it. Her father could invent a reason to bust in, but at least she'd have a split second of warning first.

Jacob inclined his head. "Princess."

"I'm not a princess, and you know it. And my father isn't really a king. Kings need subjects, and in case you haven't noticed, there are less than twenty of us in the compound. And Cary Town is a ghost town. Those days have been over for a long time."

Cary Town wasn't even protected anymore. The city's protections and organization had broken down in the fighting, and no one had bothered to put the wards back up. It was something about how too much of a magical signature might draw the magic users back. Now only a few places were protected, not the whole city. The compound was one of those places.

She'd heard the stories of her father, decades ago, how ruthless he'd been. How he'd ruled over hundreds of thousands of their kind and even therians—the shapeshifting races, striking fear into the hearts of any who would dare go against him. Now most of the vampires were dead, and those remaining had scattered, with only the most loyal few staying behind with the royal family.

Jacob peeled his shirt off so it wouldn't get blood on it. "So, what's your pleasure today, Syd? Arm? Neck?" He winked at her. "Something more risque?"

She crooked a finger at him. "Come here." Sydney sat on the edge of the bed, and Jacob joined her. She wished she felt that way about him. It would be so simple. He was attractive and kind. Even though he wasn't strong like a preternatural, she believed he would give his life to protect her. And not out of some misplaced loyalty to her dad.

"This is so wrong," she said. The past few months, the weight of what they were doing hung over her like a heavy fog.

Jacob pushed the long wavy blonde hair out of her eyes. "I love these freckles on your nose."

Sydney scrunched her face in annoyance. She'd gotten those freckles from her mother, and she wasn't nearly the fan of them Jacob seemed to be, which was another point in favor of him being smitten.

"Are you listening to me?"

"Yes," he said. "What's so wrong?" But she knew he was playing dumb and just wanted to avoid the conversation altogether.

She waved her hand around. "This! Me feeding from you. It's just... I'm using you."

He pressed a kiss against her throat. "So? Use me. I'm here at your disposal and pleasure. You have to eat, Syd."

"And then what?"

"What do you mean?"

"I'm always going to be this weak abomination that other vampires want dead. I'm always going to be a liability. What if I'm effectively immortal? Am I going to be locked away in this compound for hundreds or thousands of years? What's the point of living that way? What's the point of living at all?"

She wondered if she'd be stronger if she drank something stronger. Perhaps therian or guardian or magic user. But therians were well-hidden these days, and her father didn't have the power to capture one against their will for her feeding needs anymore. Guardians, too, had deserted. Ever since the link between heaven and earth had been severed, the fallen angels no longer feared retribution from heavenly spies for banding together. So they had.

They still guarded and took odd jobs in the preternatural world, but they only did exactly what they wanted, and their price was always high. And they absolutely refused to work for her father for any reason or price even if he had it.

Her father used to have an army of guardians that watched over her and her mother. But after the link was severed and after the war, they'd deserted, no longer fearing the king's retribution. Nobody could get fangs into a guardian without their permission, anyway.

That left magic users, but nearly all of them had stuck with their own kind—other humans—and now lived in the well-guarded human cities, ruling over the normals with their enhanced powers. The few magic users nearby all had mates, and Sydney highly doubted their mates would appreciate some weakling half-breed feeding on them.

Humans were all that was available, not that she didn't enjoy drinking from Jacob. He tasted like home and comfort—or what she imagined home might be for a normal person in another time. Not this cold, sterile compound she was kept in like some lab animal.

"I'd be really upset if you weren't here." Jacob's hand was on her shoulder. God, he was so nice, so... everything... except that he didn't make her feel that thing she thought she was supposed to feel for a man she was sleeping with.

Yeah, she was sleeping with him. If she was to be locked up like a princess in a tower, she hadn't been about to be a permanent virgin. And it wasn't as if her overprotective father would allow anyone else near her for a proper romance to bloom. One took what one could get.

She swiped at a tear as it escaped down her cheek. "You know I don't love you."

He pressed a kiss to her forehead. "I don't care. It's enough just being here with you."

"It's okay with you that you live with vampires? That

you lost your human family? That you're my dinner and after-dinner amusement? Really? That's okay with you? Because it isn't okay with me. I'm getting out of here. This is nonsense. I should have left a long time ago." She went to her closet and started tossing clothing out behind her. Jacob sat immobile as pants and tops landed on him.

"You'll die out there, Syd."

She rounded on him. "Then maybe I *should* die. Maybe it's not natural for something so weak to live at all. I wouldn't be a stress or burden on my parents, anymore. They'd get over it. They're immortal! I wouldn't be a prisoner. I'd be... free."

But would she? She'd heard the stories about heaven. The idea of going there, being in another sterile prison, scared her almost more than her current situation, but something had to change. She couldn't go on this way.

"Where will you go?" Jacob asked.

He was only humoring her. She couldn't even read minds like a normal vampire, and even she knew that. He was treating her like a child, just like her father—like some recalcitrant toddler proclaiming they were running away.

"I don't know. I don't care. Do you know I've never been outside these walls without guards? And even then I've never been more than a few blocks away. I don't even know what all of Cary Town looks like! I want to see something worth seeing."

"It's not like I get to wander much, either. Come here. You're just hungry. You need to feed."

Jacob pulled her into his arms, and she allowed

herself to melt into his warmth as he pressed her mouth against his throat. She hesitated, just breathing in his warm, clean, human scent. Dinner.

Her fangs emerged, and she bit down.

Jacob let out a hiss of pain as his muscles clenched against her bite. She wasn't even strong enough to hypnotize him into not feeling the pain. Not that a vampire could get into the head of someone else's claimed mate, anyway. She was sure when Elise fed, it didn't hurt him because of their link.

Sydney closed her eyes and pushed the thoughts away, pushed everything away but the taste of him. He patiently held her in arms that felt strong to her because she only had human strength herself.

"That's it. Just drink. It won't seem so bad after you've fed," he said as he petted her hair.

Her hands strayed down his muscled back. She felt his erection pressing into her leg. She was moments from taking his pants off and removing her own clothes, but she caught herself in time and instead ran her tongue over the wound on his throat to get the last bits of blood. She couldn't keep using him like this. Maybe feeding was necessary, but sleeping with him wasn't, and she was only leading him on, only hurting him. That wasn't who she wanted to be.

He healed, not from any healing power she had—she had none—but from Elise's claiming bite.

Outside in the hallway, someone jiggled the doorknob.

"Go away, Dad! Do I interrupt you and mom when you..."

"It's Elise."

Sydney growled and went to the door. She turned the lock and flung it open. "What?"

Elise looked past her into the room. "I'm hungry. I need my *mate*, please." She said it as if she were jealous, as if she had actual feelings for him. The claim would make her feel possessive, but Sydney knew the other vampire wasn't in love, either.

Poor Jacob. Sydney had no doubt Elise was sleeping with him, too. He was being used by both of them, and he'd never be free. Jacob seemed less thrilled to feed Elise, but he followed her out of the room without comment, his concerned gaze going back to Sydney.

She mouthed the words, "I'm fine."

He nodded, but she knew he didn't believe her. She was such a bad liar.

When they'd left, she shut the door and locked it back then turned to the pile of clothes on the bed. She filled a duffel bag with what she thought she might need, then shoved it into the back of her closet. Would Jacob tell someone? Had he even taken her seriously? She'd made empty threats of running away before. But this time, it was different.

Sydney had reached her breaking point. She felt she might die in this cage. It was bad enough that she'd never seen sunlight and would never see it—not outside a movie or photograph, anyway. She had to get out there into the world. The bag was abandoned in the closet. She needed to know where everybody was before she made her escape.

She'd need to find resting spots during the day to

shield her from the sun. If she picked wrong, she might not wake up. No, that wasn't true. She'd wake up in heaven. And no matter what they'd said about the place, it couldn't be any worse than here. Almost nothing could be worse than here.

What would she do about food? Did it even matter? Couldn't she eat wildlife? How would it be possible for her to be any more weak and useless than she already was? What difference did it make if she dined on Jacob or Bambi?

She closed the door carefully and snuck down the hall. Blue LED lights on the walls came on via motion detector as she moved past the other vampire resting chambers. Most were unoccupied these days. This level was also where they'd kept prisoners, back when there had been executions.

Sydney eased past Elise's room. Hopefully the vampire was too busy with her human to notice. From the sounds behind the door, she was distracted enough.

At the end of the lighted path was a steep set of stairs that led to the main levels. Her parents were in the living area cuddled on the couch like a couple of college sweethearts. She envied that her mother once had the option of college. Sydney had only read about it in books.

"Are you over your snit, Syd?" Anthony asked from the couch, pausing the movie they'd been watching. How could they watch the same things over and over? How could they live this way? In hiding, like so many rats. She wondered if they'd have to hide and stay in this one place if not for her. Probably not. They acted like old married people. Maybe in a way they were, but this seemed far removed from her dad's glory days.

"Hey baby," her mother said. "Do you feel better now that you've fed?"

"I don't want to talk about that with you, mom." Inappropriate.

"Sorry," Charlee said, blushing.

And now Sydney felt bad for making her mom feel bad. But she was about to make both of them feel bad if she managed the nerve to leave. She wanted to scream at the unfairness of it. Why had they let her live? Why hadn't they killed her at birth? This was no way for any of them to live. In the long run, they'd thank her for giving them their lives back.

Anthony had that look again. "He hasn't hurt you has he? I will end him if he tries." This had been his favorite conversation for the past decade.

Sydney rolled her eyes. Surely her father didn't think she was some unspoiled virgin. How old was he again? Nearly five hundred. Too old for such goofy logic.

"No, dad. He hasn't hurt me."

"Oh stop it, Anthony. Jacob is a nice man. He cares about her."

Anthony snorted. "He better watch how much he cares if he doesn't want his head removed from his body."

"Nice visual," Charlee said, smacking him in the arm then snuggling into him.

Her parents were so sickeningly sweet together.

"I'm going up to the roof."

Anthony sat straighter, alert. "Do you need me to send someone up there with you?"

"No, Dad! The whole building is warded, even the roof. I'll be fine up there." It was the only fresh air she ever got. The very idea that he was so protective that he didn't even like her on the roof alone had become too much.

"Sometimes you behave like such a child," he said.

"Oh, gee, I wonder why? Could it be that I've never been able to develop any autonomy because God forbid I get into any danger. You're such a helicopter parent."

Anthony's eyes narrowed. "Where did you learn that phrase?"

"Old sites on the Internet." Cole, The werewolf pack alpha had wired them up for Internet and electricity using the existing infrastructure and bypassing the need to pay many years ago when he and the king had been on tentative speaking terms still. Most of the hub cities used a more advanced but similar technology, but the net as it had been had become a digital wasteland to match the abandoned physical landscape.

Cole still popped by and checked things out and made sure her connection was working when her father was away.

"You don't talk about yourself to anyone on there... what you are? Who you are?"

"Of course not. Don't be ridiculous."

Her father was too paranoid.

Sydney disengaged from her parents and went to the roof. The stars were bright overhead. Not a cloud in the sky. It was breezy out, spring just starting to turn into the earliest sigh of summer.

The roof had lots of tables and an outdoor kitchen. Sometimes when it was nice they ate out there—when her father wasn't in super paranoid mode. On one end of the large roof was an Olympic-sized swimming pool. She'd had to look up *Olympic* online. The games no longer took place among the humans.

Sydney barely recalled the penthouse in the main part of town. It also had a pool on the roof. The pool here had been drained. It was too much upkeep in a world where resources were spotty at best. There were lounging chairs and beach towels where her mother and a few of the other humans at the compound liked to lie out in the sun during the day. Her mom got up a few hours before her dad so she could get some sunshine. Sydney envied her the warmth of the sun on her skin and how great that must feel to a human.

On the other end of the roof was a greenhouse hydroponic rooftop garden filled with vegetables. In Cary Town there were many months of cold weather. The greenhouse extended the growing season.

Sydney stood at the edge of the roof, wondering if she could navigate the jump. She'd never jumped that far, but it would be the easiest way out of here.

"Hey Syd!" Reynard called out from the ground. He was one of Anthony's loyal vampires. He'd been with them since before she was born. He had dark hair and thick eyebrows. With the deer carcass that was draped over his shoulders, he looked even more like a caveman than he normally did.

The vampires hunted and grew vegetables to feed their humans. Once things turned bad and the humans were herded into the cities, the vampires had kidnapped human mates when they could find one that had been banished to fend for themselves. It was how the magic users punished the common humans for crimes. They didn't bother with prisons. They simply tossed those who wouldn't play by their rules out to the monsters. No trial. No appeal.

Jacob was the only human boy she'd grown up with who she hadn't accidentally killed over the years, or who hadn't escaped and run away. If those boys could run away, so could she. Though she imagined they hadn't fared any better in the wild than she would.

Sydney went back to her room to grab her bag, the guilt of abandoning her parents clawing at her with each step. She waited until she heard everyone upstairs—except Elise and Jacob. As she passed Elise's room, the door opened.

"Where are you going?" Jacob asked.

Dammit.

"Nowhere," she said.

"Nowhere requires luggage?" He stepped out into the hallway, closing the door behind him. Elise was still in there, wrapped in a post-coital feeding glow.

"I'm leaving. I told you I was leaving. I can't stay here anymore. Just give me a head start, a few hours before you *discover* it and tell my father. I know you'll tell him."

Jacob stopped her. "I'll come with you. You need someone to look out for you. It's not safe out there."

"And what could you do to protect me? Besides, the

claim Elise has on you would lead her and my father right to me. This isn't the act of a rebellious teenager. It's the act of a desperate woman. I have to be free. I don't care if I die out there. I can't stand another minute here. Please understand."

"I understand I'm coming with you," Jacob persisted.

"Didn't you just hear me about Elise? You can't..."

"What about Elise?" The vampiress opened the door, still nude, like there had been any question of what she'd been doing while feeding. Her face held smugness as if Sydney would be jealous. What did she have to be jealous of? All she felt with regards to Jacob was guilt that she was using him to scratch the itches there was no one else around to scratch and feeding off him like he was some blood slave.

Faster than any human should be able to move, Jacob bent, removed a wooden stake from his boot, and plunged it into Elise's heart. His hand moved swiftly to his mate's mouth to cover the sound of her scream, and then she began to melt away.

Sydney's shock was quickly followed by a dark satisfaction that the bitch was gone, followed by a pang of guilt at the previous unsolicited feeling.

Jacob collapsed with the melting vampire, and for a moment, Sydney thought that the link between them, rather than freeing him and making him mortal again, had killed him as well. But he wasn't dead. Instead, he sobbed, clutching at the quickly decomposing vampire.

"Jacob, be quiet! They're going to hear and come down here!" While the walls were reinforced steel and the rooms and hallway were said to be soundproof, Jacob was having a fit over Elise, and vampire hearing was impressively good. Soundproof by human standards might not be exactly the same as soundproof by vampire standards.

He got himself together, and then Elise was nothing but bone and ash. Sydney ran down the hall to a supply closet and returned with a broom. But Jacob was too much of an emotional wreck to do anything, so Sydney swept Elise's remains under the bed. It wouldn't be long until someone needed her for something or discovered her missing.

"I thought you didn't love her?" Sydney said.

There was hope in his eyes as if her question had been fueled by jealousy instead of mere curiosity.

"I don't. But that link... it does something to you. I don't think these are my real feelings. They aren't very deep. They just scratch the surface."

If this display was just scratching the surface of Jacob's feelings, there might be issues there. Because it seemed pretty intense and epic to Sydney.

Jacob wiped his face with the back of his sleeve. "I'm fine now. There's nothing anymore. It was just the claim breaking."

She was skeptical, but his face seemed to have cleared of the mild hypnotism. Suddenly an awful thought occurred to her. "Oh God, do you think my mom doesn't love my dad? That it's just the claim?"

Jacob touched her arm. "No, Syd. It's not like that, I promise. I never wanted to be around Elise when she was alive. I didn't even like her. It was just the effect of the bond breaking. Your parents aren't like that. Charlee loves him. The claim can't create those feelings she has all the time, all it can do is create that brief surge of loss when the claim breaks. It's not even grief. Grief is deeper. It was just this brief panic and... I don't know... loss for the sake of loss. But I'm fine now. If it was your mom, trust me, she would *not* be fine in five minutes."

Sydney wasn't sure if Jacob just said it to make her feel better about what could be her mother's unremitting Stockholm syndrome. But it was true that Jacob hadn't ever followed Elise around like a lost puppy. He avoided her whenever he could, preferring to spend his time with Sydney, unlike her parents who were nearly inseparable. And just a bit icky with their public affection.

"Let's go," Jacob said, having turned an emotional one-eighty in the course of a few minutes.

"You aren't coming with me. You're too vulnerable now."

"You need someone to watch out for you and feed you."

Sydney shook her head and retreated several steps. "No. I might kill you. I don't have the greatest track record with that. Now that Elise is gone, you can die. I can't... I can't."

"You won't kill me, Syd. I have faith in you. It'll be fine."

But Sydney knew it wouldn't be fine. She might be able to control herself, but even so, she couldn't feed from him every day without him growing weak and sick. And there might not be enough out there for him to eat to help him stay strong.

"I'm eating wildlife." She pushed past him.

"I'm still coming with you," he said. "I'm dead anyway if I stay. You know the king will get into my mind. He'll kill me for letting you go."

Jacob could easily stop her. He might be only human, but he was strong for a human, and Sydney was... well Sydney. Thankfully Jacob's loyalty was with her, not her dad. Even so, she knew she had no choice but to bring him. No matter how loyal he was to her, Anthony would get inside his mind the moment they realized she was gone.

She sighed. "Fine."

He grinned. "Awesome. Let me just pack a bag real quick."

Sydney waited in the hall while Jacob packed. She didn't want to stand in Elise's room thinking about how he'd just killed a vampire without hesitation. Sure, they both had hated the bitch, but Sydney had never been faced before with the obvious moral gray Jacob had developed in all his time with vampires. Surely he must harbor some disturbing impulse toward revenge for being stolen from his family. And here he was, running off into the wilderness with the king's daughter.

Could she trust him? Maybe she should drain him the first chance she got, for her own safety.

A few minutes later he joined her, an excited, happy look on his face like they were going on a fun road trip instead of running into God only knew what was out there. "Ready?" he said.

"Yeah. No, wait." She went back to her room and took a sheet of paper and pen from her desk. She stood there, trying to come up with something that didn't sound stupid. This would kill her parents, but she was a fucking adult! Wasn't it normal for adults to move away from their parents and start their own lives?

If the old movies she'd had to sit through repeatedly were any indication, it was normal.

After a few more minutes thought she scrawled what could possibly be the lamest running away letter ever penned:

DEAR MOM AND DAD,

I'M SORRY I LEFT. *I know you'll try to come after me. Don't. Please just let me go. I can't be a locked-up princess anymore. What kind of life is that for me? I don't know how you guys stand it, but some day you'll want to be free, too. And in some small way, now you are.*

LOVE, *Syd*

SYDNEY FELT the glow come to her eyes and her fangs pop out as she growled staring at the letter. She sounded like she was fifteen. She *had* to get out of here before she regressed back to toddler. She folded the paper and left it on the desk and followed Jacob down the hall. The blue LED lights clicked on as they approached and clicked off as they receded.

They climbed the steep stairs and went down a

couple of other hallways. She heard her mother laughing at something stupid her father said and almost lost her nerve. But her life might be measured in centuries, and eternity here wasn't an option.

"Syd, you okay?" Jacob whispered.

"Fine. Let's go."

Jacob led her out a back door on the main level, away from the sounds of the deer being dressed and prepared in the large kitchen. A lot of that meat would be stored for winter.

The two of them stood outside under the bright moon with the mild near-summer breeze blowing over them. Thousands of stars were visible, all twinkling and unassuming. This was the same view she'd had on the roof more or less. But down here, outside the protection of the compound, it felt different. More wild. More free.

With each step they took farther from the big metal building, Sydney's guilt grew. She'd get Jacob killed, and herself as well. But she kept walking, and he kept walking.

"I know where there's a car. We can travel more safely that way than on foot," Jacob said.

Sydney had never ridden in a car—that she could remember, anyway. She was sure at some point in her babyhood before the world had changed that she must have, but it was too long ago.

"What will we do when the sun rises?"

"We'll find a place. There are a lot of abandoned houses now from when the people moved into the cities. Some of them have basements. We'll be fine. We just need to get on the road."

"Jacob, why are you helping me?" He seemed too eager. What if he was leading her to danger? Could she trust him when she fell dead for the day unprotected? He'd put the stake back into his boot after killing Elise, as if he might need it later. For her?

"You know how I feel about you," he said. "You know I'd do anything for you."

His hand was warm in hers as he took it and led her off to the car that would take them far from everything that had ever been safe.

2

Noah paced in the glass magic-reinforced cage. It was a hundred square feet, not nearly enough room for a wolf. The door slid open and raw meat was shoved in. He felt the glow come to his eyes, and he shifted. Raw meat was better in wolf form.

He shouldn't shift. Any time he did, they just took more blood to use in their magic. The meat was drugged to sedate him so he wouldn't struggle or hurt them when they brought out the needle. But sometimes oblivion was a good thing. It allowed him to dream about the good times when he was a pup.

He ripped into the meat, barely tasting the drugs. Whatever it was, it didn't seem to have long term effects on his strength or health. Maybe it wasn't a drug. Maybe it was a potion. It had an herbal flavor.

When the plate was clean, Noah drifted to the corner, the lethargy overtaking him. And he did dream.

He was seven or eight, right before he'd been taken.

He'd been born in his fur and had only had a human form for about three years by that point. He still felt gangly and awkward as a human. It felt unnatural after spending so long living on four legs. It was as if the wolf was him and the human was what he shapeshifted into. Instead of the reverse.

He played under the sun with his den mates. The war was going on. It had been going on forever. But the hive and the surrounding forests and fields had been well-protected by a witch called Tam and a sorcerer named Dayne, along with a few others of their kind.

They were the only magical beings that reminded Noah that not all the magic users were bad. They weren't all on the human side in the war.

Noah laid in the sun stretching his arms way out so he could be more tan like his dad. "Hey Mom, where's Sydney? Why can't she ever come out and play with me?" He didn't understand why Sydney didn't go in the sun like he did. The sun was great.

"She can't, honey," Jane said. "She has an allergy. You can see her when the sun goes down."

"Great!" He ran to the stream to watch his den mates to see if they could catch a fish right out of the water with fangs and paws.

Syd was his best friend. He was going to protect her and take care of her forever.

His dad had seemed skeptical of that but wouldn't tell him why except that, "The king would never allow it."

Well, he wasn't Noah's king, so screw that. Sydney

was too awesome to have that big angry vampire for a dad, anyway.

A black cat came out of nowhere and pounced on him, then ran back into the woods. Aunt Greta. One of these days he or one of the others might accidentally hurt her. But the werecat was fast! So maybe not. His dad chuckled from under a nearby tree.

Moments later, Greta emerged from the forest in some jeans and a T-shirt. She had clothes stashed in the woods all over the place. None of the wolves cared about being naked, but Aunt Greta was different. His mom called her *reserved*.

"Hey Jane," she said, "Anthony's being all crazy again. Let's go kidnap Charlee for some girl time while he's asleep. She needs to get out of that compound before she loses her mind."

His mom stood and stretched then bent to kiss his dad. "I'm game."

"Be careful," Cole said. Like he needed to say that to Noah's bad ass demon mom. Nobody could hurt Jane. She could make herself where she was like a ghost, and you couldn't even touch her. And she had this scary demon form that sometimes Noah saw when he didn't clean his cave. And she could shift into anything. She could become a bird and fly away. She was his hero.

"Careful is my middle name, babe," she said. Before she left with Aunt Greta she turned back to Noah. "*You* be careful. Stay safe."

Noah rolled his eyes at his mother. "Mom, I am the most powerful of all the werewolves that ever lived. I mean look at these muscles!" He held his arms up. They looked like regular kid arms and not the superpowered child he seemed to believe he was.

"Yeah, you are!" his dad said, chuckling.

Jane just shook her head, a wry grin on her face. "Just be careful."

Noah jolted out of the dream, finding himself back in the sterile glass room. He whimpered and put his nose between his paws. He should have listened to his mother, and he still blamed himself for it. He'd only been a pup, but he still should have listened. He'd been old enough to listen. Even if he couldn't manage it as listening to his parents, he should have listened to them as the pack alphas. No one else his age had gotten free passes like that. The alpha's word was law to the pack.

It wasn't long after that he'd been taken. He'd been playing chicken with the protected areas versus the unprotected areas with his friends. He'd jumped outside the protections at just the wrong moment and been taken by some magic users.

And he'd been here ever since.

Noah stretched and stood. Even more than being kept a prisoner, he hated that his blood might be used for magic to hurt more preternaturals. From what he could see, the humans had protected themselves well in tightly-controlled fortress cities. Now they were being aggressive because they could.

New clothes had been neatly folded and placed in the center of his cell. He shifted back to his human form and stretched again, then he ambled to the center of the room. He winked at the camera high in the wall over his cell. It was a holographic square patch that blended well into the glass, but he could still see it. Noah wasn't sure if humans could detect it, but his vision was more enhanced than that. He could see the iridescent ripple that proved it wasn't the same as the surrounding glass. He wasn't sure if it was technology or magic. Over the past decade the two had blurred together until one was indistinguishable from the other.

He dressed, then sat and waited. It felt like hours passed, but it was probably less than half of one when a cheery robotic feminine voice in the ceiling said: "Number 5856, Please prepare to exit your cell for daily exercise."

"Noah," he whispered under his breath.

He looked at the numbered tattoo on his upper arm. It was the same place his dad's alpha tattoo was. Just more insult added to injury. When he busted out of this shit hole, he'd get it tattooed over with something closer to what Cole had. Each day when he heard 5856, he whispered "Noah" so he wouldn't forget. After twenty years in captivity, they'd already made him forget his last name. He couldn't allow the same to happen with his first.

The glass door slid open with a whoosh, and a gust of cool canned air hit him in the face, filling him with a sense of wellness and happiness. But Noah wasn't fooled. It was the stuff they put in the air conditioning to keep everybody calm. He was sure the humans in the main city were getting dosed with it as well to keep everyone docile and obedient.

For all he knew it actually worked on them. He wasn't sure if it worked on the other preternatural prisoners, but no matter what Noah's emotional side said, the cool, logical part of him wasn't buying into it.

He barely remembered the machinations of the vampire king when he'd been building up his police state before the magic users had started taking over. But if Anthony could see this? He'd get a hard on. The humans had proven to be more diabolical than vampires. And that was saying something. Congrats, humans!

He filed out with the other numbered therian prisoners into the hallway. The cell next to his, 5857, was empty tonight. It wasn't the first time a prisoner had disappeared and never returned. Noah tried not to think about it.

"Please follow the glowing arrows to the exercise yard, and remember to play nice with your friends."

Noah hid the eye-roll. It would do him no favors for the cameras to catch a whiff of rebellion. He moved quietly with the inmates from nearby cells down the seemingly never-ending hallway. Another door slid open that took them into the exercise yard, which was a giant balcony instead of a real yard.

Even so, out here he could feel the moon on his face. He hadn't seen the sun in more years than he could count because his group was mixed in with vampires now. But it only made him think of Sydney and how she'd never seen the sun.

Noah's complexion was naturally dark, so at least he didn't look too sickly. But he still missed the sunlight.

Someday.

Somehow in everything he'd lost, he'd managed to retain the memory of the date of his birth. Occasionally, he asked one of the guards what day it was. He'd been keeping up with the year as well. It wouldn't be long now.

His twenty-eigth birthday had just passed. The next full moon he would reach his full power. If there was any chance at all, it would be on that night.

He'd forgotten about the twenty-eighth birth moon. But one day in a dream after he'd eaten the drugged meat, Aunt Greta of all people had shown up, telling him the harrowing story of what her twenty-eighth birth moon had been like.

It could have just been a dream, but when he woke, he remembered. Aunt Greta wasn't mated in the same way his kind or the demons or vampires were mated, but she lived with a man who was much the same as a mate, a sorcerer named Dayne. Had he somehow made it possible for the werecat to deliver the message? Or was it a coincidence—his own subconscious reminding him that there might be a way to escape this place after all?

Was somebody out there still hoping and believing Noah was alive? He wanted to believe they hadn't given up on him.

In the early years, he'd only been a child. The idea of escape had seemed like a lofty dream. It was a comforting story he told himself to fall asleep, and then, once asleep, it became more real and played out in vivid color.

But each day when he woke, it became the impossible feat once again. These people were powerful. They'd created a fortress of their city that no preternatural could get inside, and a fortress of their prisons that no preternatural could get out of.

As he'd grown older and wiser, he'd begun to see the cracks in their security, the way they believed too much in the stuff they sent in with the canned air, the drugs they gave them, the cheery robotic voice that worked daily to brainwash a bit more of their soul away.

Noah wouldn't let them succeed. He thought about his parents, about Aunt Greta, about Sydney. He trained his mind daily to stay stronger than his captors even if he seemed obedient, even if it seemed he would never attempt escape because he never had before.

"Please remember, keep fraternizing to a minimum while in the fitness yard," the cheerful robotic voice said over loud speakers. The speakers sat atop very tall fences crowned with barbed wire.

Noah didn't have to shift yet under the moon, but when it was full, he wouldn't have much of a choice—particularly on his twenty-eighth birth moon. One would think if it was the night he'd reach the height of his power that he'd be able to control the shift when under the moon, but it didn't quite work that way. The moon overwhelmed most of them, even the strongest, unless they'd just fed.

He ran laps around the yard. They didn't have to tell him not to fraternize. Others would betray you when it would save their own neck or when it most suited them. If you told someone your thoughts or feelings or plans, they were out there. And in a place like this, that was bad. He wouldn't speak to anyone, and was only grateful that as a werewolf, nobody could force their way inside his mind.

They watched all therian interactions closely. But they didn't worry about Noah and had long ago figured out that he wasn't about to form any tight bonds. In their minds, it probably meant he'd succumbed to his fate— accepted it so he wasn't a threat to them. In his own it meant he didn't have to worry about busting anybody else out to take with him.

He wouldn't allow himself to get attached. To any of them. He'd have one shot, and friends would only be dead weight.

SYDNEY SAT in the passenger side while Jacob drove. She still wished she could have left him at the compound, but he was a dead man either way he went: coming out here into the wild with her or staying behind.

It was only a matter of which way he wanted to die, and he seemed to have chosen with Sydney. If it might be any consolation to the human driving the old-fashioned truck, she'd be killed right along with him. He was stronger than her, and a better fighter. So if he died, she did. Unless she accidentally drained him first.

When the humans had reinforced the cities against the preternaturals, they'd used magic to find new technologies and then blended the two into an almost seamless whole. Suddenly they had no need or use for fossil fuels. Nobody cared about them anymore. Oil fields had been abandoned all over the world.

The remaining preternaturals had taken it upon themselves to gain control of them because some might need to travel long distances using vehicles left behind. Automobile companies outside the major cities were taken over as well, creating a slow but steady trickle of new vehicles to replace the old ones that wore out.

The truck Sydney and Jacob were in was an old green beater that had managed to last over twenty years, which made it dinosaur-old in car age. It had been well cared for, even if the sides of it were rusting. Jacob had found it pretty easily at an abandoned service station in the middle of Cary Town—a service station that some intrepid rebel had made a gasoline delivery to.

The entire town had crumbled like some post-apoca-lyptic nightmare without enough people to keep things running. But Sydney still had the vaguest memory of her father's penthouse at the Cary Town Luxury Apartments, before he'd relocated them permanently to the compound.

"Whatcha thinking about, Syd?" Jacob asked. His hand drifted to her knee, and she shifted closer to the window.

She was now keenly aware of the danger Jacob posed. Sure, they'd slept together before, and deep down she knew he hadn't had much of a choice in the matter. He'd been their blood slave, and neither she nor Elise had been particularly shy about utilizing his other charms.

But Sydney had never tried to force herself on him. She couldn't have anyway, but maybe, with her father being who he was, the threat had been implied if the princess was made unhappy. That thought horrified her.

She hoped Jacob hadn't seen it that way, but now wasn't the best time to bring the conversation up. Not when they were on a deserted road, and he was the most powerful being within screaming distance.

"Nothing," she replied.

"Come on, that isn't the face of somebody thinking about nothing."

"I was just thinking about how everything has changed so much." They'd been driving for hours, and she'd fought not to think much about her parents or how they would feel about all this. But she'd been suffocating there. They had to understand. Weren't they suffocating, too?

But her parents had seemed happy. Instead of hating the confinement, her dad especially had seemed sedate most of the time. The pressures of being king had faded once he lost control of everything. It was as if he'd found some zen place now that he couldn't micromanage the entire world.

He'd been content to micromanage Sydney instead. It was an uncharitable thing to think about her father. He worried about her.

As long as he knew his mate and daughter were safe, he seemed happy. He was very different from the Anthony Burgess she'd heard stories about. It made her wonder if they were even all true.

"Maybe we should go back," Sydney said, already regretting her decision. She could negotiate something less restrictive with her father. He loved her. Maybe he could be reasoned with. Though, by the time she got back, her dad would be so livid she might be confined to not just the compound, but her room as well, under guard until he calmed down. And with a vampire, that could be months.

He wasn't known to let go of grudges. He'd been obsessed for years with finding out where the Cary Town pack's den was. When he'd finally discovered the den, it didn't matter anymore. Things had spiraled well past the point where he could control anything. Sydney used to play with the alpha wolf's pup.

Noah hadn't shifted to human for the first time until he was five, and it was so weird for her that Sydney didn't see him for a few weeks after that because she couldn't understand why he had turned into a boy. After he disappeared a few years later, she'd become despondent, and her father had gotten even crazier about the wards and protections and never letting her out of his sight.

Jacob drove faster. Not exactly the response she was expecting to "Maybe we should go back." His face was tense.

"Syd... we're not going back."

"But..." Maybe he was right. Maybe she should keep going. But wasn't that supposed to be her decision? She'd let him tag along and now he was acting like he was the one in charge.

"I'm sorry, Syd. I need to go back to my family."

"Okay, so go, but take me home, first."

"I wish it were that simple. I don't know where they are. But I know someone who does. We've orchestrated a trade." It was clear from the expression on his face that she was the trade.

"What? How? You live with *vampires*!" Sydney didn't

understand how Jacob could possibly be some kind of double agent. Wouldn't a vamp have seen inside his head? The others couldn't read him with Elise's claim on him. But Elise could. Then again, the vampiress had harbored a strong grudge against Sydney for a while now. It wouldn't have been hard to get her cooperation.

"I met some magic users from the Hub City."

It used to be known as Las Vegas a long time ago, but when it was taken over by magic users, it had become the central point of organization in this country.

"And?" She kept hoping for a punchline. She was afraid she might be the punchline.

"And, they know where my parents are. They shielded my mind so when I killed Elise, none of the other vamps would have a chance to read me and know what was happening. I'm sorry. They said they want to study you. They're fascinated by what you are."

And here she'd been worried about *his* safety. What completely wasted angst.

Sydney wiped away a stray tear. It was bad enough to be so physically weak, but she couldn't let him see her cry on top of everything else. "I thought you loved me."

"I find you attractive, and you aren't unlikeable. It wasn't hard to pretend what I wanted you to see. But you had to know I wouldn't be happy after being taken from my family like that. The other humans at the compound are different. They fell for the vampires who claimed them because they were thrown out of the cities to the monsters, and those monsters have treated them well in the end. It's a little harder for me to romanticize it."

She was glad she'd never fallen for him. It was bad

enough to be betrayed by someone she'd thought was a friend. If she'd thought of him as more it would have been crushing. At least she didn't have to be the foolish girl who fell in love with him.

"I'm going to start looking for a resting place for you for the day. I'll figure out what I'm going to eat when you're asleep."

Once the sun came up, she'd sleep like the dead, literally. She wouldn't rise until after sunset. And Sydney rose later than many other vampires, anyway. There were so many stupid ways in which she was different, weaker, and not any kind of respectable vampire at all.

"What am I going to eat?" she asked.

"Me, like always," he said with a smirk that left her disgusted. Before, it had been bearable. Now, the idea of drinking his blood when he intended to give her to the humans made her want to vomit.

The feeling of revulsion didn't last. Something predatory came over her, and she was filled with calm. Perhaps there was some remnant buried deep inside her of what she was meant to be as a vampire. She wasn't sure what this feeling that had bubbled up meant, but she was going to drain every last drop of blood out of him. And then she was going home.

"I didn't want you to find out like this," he said, not having noticed the change in her demeanor.

"No, because this makes it awkward. You might have to feel guilty. It would have been so much easier if little Sydney hadn't asked any questions until the transaction started. Do I have it about right?"

Jacob turned red, and Sydney thought she could

convince him not to do it. But the things she'd end up doing with him in order to have the smallest chance, turned her stomach. No, she was killing the shithead. She'd worry about what she'd eat on the way home.

He was quiet for a long time, only the sound of the old truck piercing the silence. What else was left to say? The rest of the drive, Sydney spent fantasizing about what would have happened if she'd gotten away on her own—if she hadn't confided in the human.

Her father might not have been able to get into Jacob's head with the magic that cloaked and protected him, but when he discovered Elise's remains he would have known something was wrong and would have gotten the information out of him the old-fashioned way. Then he would have carved Jacob up like the game the others hunted.

It was a nice fantasy, but she needed to focus. She was already getting sleepy. It didn't even take the sun coming up to wear her out. Even normal vampires couldn't get up when the sun was in the sky, but that went double for Syndey.

They were in Oregon now. She'd seen signs on the road they'd driven on. The Hub City was in Nevada. Sydney wasn't sure if he was taking her the whole way or if they'd meet someone else who would take her. If she planned to kill him, this might be her only opportunity.

They'd passed a place called "Bend" about an hour ago. It was deserted like most other places. Or else those who lived there were in hiding, hoping the cities had lost interest in them.

Jacob pulled off the road when he spotted a farmhouse. Sydney contemplated running, but he'd catch her, and she knew he'd picked an area like this intentionally. It was so much wide open space, hundreds of acres. The only safe place for her when the sun came up would be inside that farmhouse somewhere. Or maybe the nearby barn.

"Let's go inside and find you a safe space."

Such an odd thing for him to say right now, but he would want her safe for the trade. If she died, she was no good to him and he couldn't get back to his precious family. It made Sydney feel even more guilty for trying to escape hers.

She wondered if someone had delivered the truck and left it for him for the drive. She wondered what other things he'd been planning. He probably had non-perishable food already packed away in the back of the truck, shipped to him by humans. *Figuring out* what he'd eat likely just meant deciding on a canned meat and vegetable, not hunting something as she'd previously imagined.

As she followed him into the house, she envisioned jumping on his back and sinking her fangs into his throat, draining him so fast he couldn't react, but she knew he'd toss her right off him. And then she'd be screwed.

No, she had to wait until he offered her his vein and distract him so she could drink more than she should. It had been so long since she'd drank too much from him —so long since it had been a real threat. In the decade since Elise had claimed him, he'd probably forgotten how weak he could get from blood loss and how fast.

Jacob opened cabinets in the kitchen, and a white mouse scurried by squeaking in irritation. A few cans of food in the pantry had exploded after years and years of sitting expired in a house with no temperature control.

"No one has been here since the original owners. And from the looks of it, they haven't been here in a long time, either."

His boots creaked over the rotting hardwood as he went down the hallway. Sydney silently prayed the floor would collapse and he'd break his neck falling into a basement, but it didn't happen. He reached the end safely.

She stood in the hall, not liking close proximity with this Jacob. His head popped out again a few minutes later. "Bedroom in here, Syd. There's a big, empty closet you can sleep in. I just have to cover this hole in the wood so the sun doesn't get you."

There was a large picture window directly across from the closet door that looked like it probably got some direct sunlight. As resting places went, this was far less secure than she'd like, but she had to be breathing for this *trade* to happen. Barring a freak raid on the place, she knew she'd make it at least until night in the closet.

He went back down the hall, leaving her in the bedroom. She heard doors opening and closing and banging around in drawers until he returned with shiny silver tape. He got a look of longing in his eyes.

"My dad used to have this. It's duct tape. You can fix anything with it." He covered the hole in the wood, then sat on the edge of the bed and tossed the tape on the floor.

Sydney pushed back the revulsion that went through her as he rolled back his sleeve. And then she thought, *Great, he won't let me near his neck.* It would be harder to kill him this way.

She sat beside him and sank her fangs into the offered arm. Her hand inched up the inside of his leg, but then Jacob's hand was on top of hers, stilling her.

"As good as you can make me feel, Syd, I know you're just trying to sway me. It can't be done. I'm going back to my family, and you'll never see yours again. I'm sorry this is the way it had to go down. I'm sorry you come from a family of monsters and must suffer for their crimes."

She cringed as his hand stroked through her hair. But then, he started telling the most insipid stories about his childhood before the vampire king had him brought to the compound to be on Sydney's dinner menu. He wasn't paying close attention to her feeding or how much time had elapsed.

If he just kept talking... After a few minutes, his words began to slur and slow as he stumbled and tripped over sentences. This could work! She could taste freedom. A moment later, she felt a sharp zap of electricity, and then she blacked out.

SYDNEY WOKE, feeling weaker than normal, even though she'd fed a lot. She struggled out of the closet she'd been carelessly tossed into to find an angry Jacob sitting on the edge of the bed, a black rectangular box in his hand.

He looked down at it, then back at her. "Just some

protection that was sent to me with the truck and provisions."

Provisions. Yes, there was food in the back of the truck. Far from roughing it, they'd provided her captor with everything he needed to comfortably transport the vampire cargo. Her attention went back to the weapon on his lap.

"I didn't want to have to use it. You knew you were taking too much. Shame on you, Syd."

"Shame on me?" She was only trying to survive. She wasn't the one he had a conflict with. It wasn't like she'd picked him out of a catalog, or like she'd known how her father had secured her meals. She'd been too young to think through the ramifications of any of that.

She felt gross from sleeping in the closet, and she wondered how many of those field mice had crawled over her in her sleep. She wondered if Jacob had done anything inappropriate while she'd been unconscious. And then she started to cry, because what was the point anymore of pretending to be brave?

A hint of guilt shone from his eyes, but he just said, "We need to get back on the road."

He dragged her to the truck and made sure she was buckled in. This time he didn't hide the fact that he had plenty of food for the trip. He took a dried meat product in a plastic wrapper and a canned beverage from the back and got into the truck.

Sydney was hungry, but she knew he wouldn't let her feed again until they stopped. And she also knew the black box would be poised and ready in case she tried anything else stupid.

3

Noah sat in a corner of the glass cell. An hour maybe until exercise time. The moon was getting closer. Tonight more than any other time before, he felt amped up, like he couldn't run enough. He'd already been tempted on his laps around the yard to shift, but if he did it before the full moon it would look suspicious.

The twenty-eighth birth moon was the most important and special day for a therian. He should have been with his family, celebrating. As the alpha's son, the whole pack would have gone all out for a huge party. Even with how the world had changed, they would make something special. He would have shifted and gone running with them all, fed, and then come back to party some more.

He'd been to a twenty-eighth birth moon celebration when he was just a pup, right after he'd shifted to human for the first time, and though he'd had to go to bed early since he was so young, and a lot of the party was more adult-centered, he'd remembered the buzz in the air, the excitement, and how he couldn't wait until his own twenty-eighth birth moon.

It wasn't turning out quite like he'd thought it would. Though now, it was even more exciting, because it might mean freedom and reuniting with his family, assuming he could find his way back home.

Noah went through the mental checklist of his escape plan. He'd been forming it casually for years, but only more specifically for the past three months. He was deep in thought when he smelled her through the glass of his cell. The sweetest smell in the universe.

His nostrils flared. It couldn't be.

But it was.

He would never forget that scent if he lived to be two thousand. That scent was burned into his brain. That scent was Sydney.

"5856, congratulations, you have a new neighbor. Meet 5857B. Isn't she pretty?" The cheery robotic voice emphasized the letter B too harshly, as if to say, *Yes, 5857 is dead. We killed him. This one might be next. Perhaps there will be a 5856B as well.*

Not if Noah had anything to say about it. He growled and looked down at his tattoo. If they laid a hand on her... If they marked her in any way... He began to pace in the far-too-small cell as a rage he'd never before felt began to build.

∽

SYDNEY RETREATED to the other end of the glass cube, her back pressed against the farthest wall she could get from the angry, growling guy with glowing, yellow eyes. Fur began to sprout on his arms and fangs pushed through his gums. A voice came out over the speakers.

"Be polite, 5856. We would like this one to last a while."

Polite, yeah right. But the fur disappeared back into his skin. The fangs receded, and his eyes went back to a normal brown. She wasn't sure how strong the glass was. Was it shatterproof? Was she about to find out? What was he?

He could be any number of therian breeds but something inside her screamed "werewolf". But the wolves she remembered as a kid had all been nice. Not like this.

Had he killed the last person in the cube she now occupied? How had he gotten in? Had they let him in? So many questions and way too much intense staring aimed at her.

A few minutes passed, and someone in a white lab coat came to her door. The glass slid open. The woman in the coat had a friendly smile, but Sydney didn't trust it. Despite her recent road trip, she wasn't *that* gullible. She knew the score now.

She sniffed the air. Human. Magical human. She'd never had blood from a magic user before, and she was sure she wasn't about to get it now. The only kind of blood she'd ever had was regular human. It was all they'd been able to get.

"5857B, if you'll come with me please."

"S-Sydney. M-my name is Sydney."

"5857B," the woman repeated, glancing at the clipboard in her hand as if it contained all infallible knowledge. "Please, let's not make this difficult."

Sydney looked back to see 5856 growling some more and followed the woman in the white coat out of the cube. Between the two, she seemed to be the safer option.

She was grateful for the silence as they walked down the hall. It allowed her to digest everything.

Jacob had taken no chances with her and had always had the weapon ready in case she tried any further pathetic escape or murder attempts. She couldn't even kill a regular human who'd practically shoved her fangs into his vein. What an awful excuse for a vampire she was.

Tonight had been a shorter drive. The night was only just now reaching its midpoint. She knew because she felt her strongest in the middle of the night. But she was so hungry. The traveling and stress had worn on her.

She'd begged Jacob to reconsider. She'd offered to help him find his family, even though she had no idea who they were or where they could be or how to get the information to find them. She'd even suggested that maybe the magic users he'd met didn't know either. Maybe it was a trick. Maybe they just wanted her and were using the story they knew would most easily gain his cooperation. Maybe they were even a danger to him.

Stories had filtered out from the human cities. The human mates at the compound had all been *criminals* who'd been thrown out into the wilderness—to the monsters—for their disobedience. But they had never seemed particularly criminal to Sydney. Just scared. They'd expected the monsters to rip them apart or torture them. It was the kind of story talked about in hushed whispers in the cities. It was why they never tried to escape their prison even though the only barriers keeping them in was the fear of being thrown out. The real barriers were to keep the preternaturals from coming in and getting to the easy food and resources.

Vampires had been lying in wait for all of them as soon as they'd been tossed out. They'd never stopped to consider that, given how hard food was to come by, that they would be protected and cherished, not abused.

But Jacob's story was different. He'd been taken from his family before things had gotten terrible. He hadn't been tossed out as a criminal. He must have been so scared of the vampires.

She'd gotten Jacob to entertain the notion that the human cities might not follow through on their side of the deal. It was a few brief minutes in which her hope had overcome her fear, but then his face had hardened and he was back to his mission, his foot pressed more firmly against the gas than before. He'd been determined to deliver her to her fate.

The trade had been fast. Her, for a folded up piece of paper with an address. As two men in white coats had escorted her toward a steel tunnel, Jacob had said. "Syd, I'm sorry."

She hadn't looked back. She wouldn't acknowledge him or give him the barest hint that there would ever be a point in time in which she could forgive him for this.

"5857B?" The woman said, snapping a finger in front of Sydney's face. "We're here."

The room looked like a hospital room Sydney had seen once on an old movie her parents had in their collection. She panicked as the woman pulled her into the room.

"Relax. It's nothing to be afraid of. We just need to run some tests. We know who you are and what you are. We'd like to know if you've stopped aging."

Sydney calmed and allowed herself to be led into the room. She'd like to know that, too. The big question had always been whether or not she would age and die, or if she could potentially be immortal. She knew, of course, that she could never be immortal. She wasn't strong like her father or other regular vampires. She was far too fragile and easy to kill, too weak to defend herself against anything. So no, she wouldn't be immortal. Something would take her out eventually and free those who loved her from their constant vigilance.

But she wanted to know if she'd stopped aging, or if her aging process had slowed somehow. She didn't think she looked twenty-seven, but then, some women aged better than others, and she'd never know how her mother might have aged. Charlee had been frozen at twenty-six when she'd been claimed by Anthony.

The woman in the coat guided Sydney to a medical examining table.

"Sit here and roll back your sleeve. We're just going to take some blood and a tissue sample."

"T-tissue sample?" Sydney's mind went straight to terrible things involving scalpels.

"Just a swab inside your cheek." The woman patted her on the arm and smiled kindly. Aside from insisting on calling Sydney by a number and a letter instead of her real name, she seemed non-threatening, nice even. But Sydney shook the thought from her head. They were only being nice to try to gain her trust. Just as Jacob had. There was no reason to think people who would lock you in a cell and run experiments on you were "nice people".

Sydney's eyes went to the vein pulsing in the woman's throat. At least she couldn't hear the blood rushing through like a real vampire would have, or the heartbeat. It might have driven her to do something stupid. Thankfully she could only see the twitch of the vein.

"You're hungry," the woman said, conversationally.

Maybe if Sydney were a real vampire, that thought would have struck some fear in the technician, but instead she went for a cotton swab.

"Open."

Sydney opened her mouth and the woman took a sample and put it into a plastic bag.

"I'll tell you what," she said, "I'll take your blood, then I'll give you some blood in return."

Sydney felt the glow come to her eyes, and she nodded. Now that she was an adult, she preferred to drink from men. It wasn't like that for all vampires. Some women preferred other women, and some men other men. It seemed tied directly into who they were attracted to, but she was too hungry right now to care much about that distinction.

She winced and bit her lip as the needle went into

her arm and the woman drew a couple of vials of blood and put labels on them.

"There. That wasn't so bad was it? It's time to go back now."

"But..." Were they lying to her already?

"Your food will be waiting for you when you return to your cell. You know the way. Don't go exploring. We'll know." The woman pressed a button and the door to the room they were in opened. She went back to her clipboard jotting down notes.

Sydney wanted to run, but how? To where? And she was so very tired suddenly. She could sleep for a million years and yet, they'd just reached the night's peak. Glowing arrows illuminating the glass guided her back to her cell.

When she reached the glass cube, the door opened and a perky robotic voice said: "Welcome home, 5857B."

She winced. Home? Yeah right. This would never be home. It would end up being her coffin, if anything.

Inside the cube was a table with a few clear medical bags filled with red fluid. What the hell was this? Bagged blood? She couldn't live on bagged blood. It was so weak, she'd probably die of malnourishment if she drank it—if such a thing was possible for a vampire.

She circled the bag a couple of times, a grimace on her face. This would be disgusting, like her mother's stories of old ladies eating canned cat food.

She looked up to find the scary growly guy in the cube next to hers watching her intently. She wished he would stop that. It freaked her out.

She picked up one of the bags and turned away from

him. There were glass cubes containing a preternatural on all four sides of her—if you didn't count the hallway outside the door—as well as above and below her. It wasn't as if she would get any feeding privacy here, but the way he watched her was too intense. The cubes were lined up and stacked on top of each other. She was on one of the higher floors as there seemed to be far more cubes below than above. It created an odd sense of vertigo, like somehow the glass would stop holding her and she'd just fall. But maybe that was the hunger talking.

She allowed the glow to come to her eyes and her fangs to descend, then she took a deep breath and bit into the bag. She was right. It was disgusting. It was cold and dead. There wasn't even the smallest trace of an emotion in it. This would keep her going about as well as weeds in the backyard would keep a human going.

But she persisted and drank down the other two bags in quick succession, trying not to taste the terrible swill.

She turned to find a giant platter of raw meat had been placed inside the other guy's cell. Then the mystery of what kind of therian he was, was solved. A reddish-brown and white wolf rolled and tumbled out of the plain white clothing they wore in the cubes, then he devoured the meat. He seemed to be enjoying his food much more than Sydney had enjoyed hers. Maybe it would divert his attention away from her.

After he'd cleaned the plate, he went to a corner and curled up and promptly fell asleep. Minutes later, some lab coats came in. One drew some of his blood into a vial much like had been done earlier with her, though she suspected this was for a different purpose.

If this place was run by magic users, the therians were having their blood stolen for use in magic. The second technician snipped some fur and put it into a plastic bag. Yes, they were using it for magic. Unless he was new, too, and they were running tests on his genetic makeup. But somehow Sydney thought they weren't as interested in a run-of-the-mill werewolf as they were in her freakish self.

A couple of hours passed. Every now and then the wolf twitched like he was having a dream. During this time, another lab coat came in and took his old clothes away, replacing them with fresh folded clothes.

Sydney watched the preternaturals in the cubes below her. A lot of them paced. Some slept while lab techs took blood. Some were agitated. Others seemed resigned to their fates. How long had they all been in here? How long would she be in here?

When the wolf woke, he prowled the cube, pacing back and forth, watching her in wolf form for several minutes. Hadn't the raw meat been enough to take the predatory edge off? She stayed in the far corner of her cube, trying to remain as far from him as possible, but somehow she knew he could smell her through the glass. And if she were any kind of proper vampire, she would have been able to smell him, too.

She should be more distressed by the general situation, but the anxiety over the wolf had been successfully distracting her over all the possible threats to her safety here. The magical humans were the real enemy. She knew that. But it was hard to keep that thought in the forefront of her mind when the wolf kept growling and watching her like she was a bone he wanted to gnaw on.

Finally, the tension eased and he shifted back to his far-too-gorgeous human form. This guy had to be working out somehow because nature didn't just give somebody muscles like that. Jacob had spent hours in the compound's gym every week, and yet even he hadn't been this delicious-looking.

Sydney's hand flew to her mouth when she realized her fangs had popped out. Did she want to sleep with him or have him for dinner?

Yes.

He wasn't the only predator here. Too bad nature hadn't given her anything to back that up with.

The werewolf noticed her gawking and came to the edge of his cube, the closest he could get to her. He stood in all his naked glory staring her down until she averted her eyes. *God, Syd, what is wrong with you?*

If the attraction were mutual, maybe he wouldn't try to break through the glass and maul her, but the hard look in his eyes gave her little hope of that. She glanced surreptitiously through the veil of her blonde hair to watch him turn and move to his clothes in the center of his cube. She tried unsuccessfully not to ogle his back and his ass and the back of his thighs. *Stop, Syd!*

She was stopped from further angering the wolf or embarrassing herself beyond repair by the too-happy robotic voice.

"Number 5857B, please prepare to exit your cell for daily exercise."

The glass door on her cube slid open. But then, so did the door to the right of her... 5856. The wolf. His eyes glowed as he glanced over. *Oh shit. Oh shit. Oh shit.* There was no longer any barrier stopping him from coming into her cube. Was that how the previous occupant had gone out? It hadn't been lost on her that the wolf was just 5856 and she was 5857B. They weren't exactly subtle around here.

But then warm air that smelled like raspberries hit her in the face, and suddenly for some reason she felt very calm and peaceful.

The robotic voice spoke again: "Please follow the glowing arrows to the exercise yard, and remember to play nice with your friends."

The word *friends*, snapped her out of the calm enough to think *yeah, right*. She wasn't sure why she'd had that mental break for a second where everything was roses and chocolate hearts, but she was mostly back to normal. The tension of moving in a single file line with the rest of the preternaturals who were far stronger than her was more than enough to shake any sense of peace she'd felt.

She followed the glowing arrows and the werewolf in front of her. His white T-shirt practically glowed against his olive skin. Just underneath where the fabric ended on his arm was a black tattoo with the number 5856. Sydney guessed it hadn't been a voluntary tattoo and was thankful she didn't have one. Yet.

As they walked down the hallway, she couldn't help being mesmerized by the way his muscles moved under the shirt as he walked. She wanted to lick... no bite... no stroke...

The wolf in front of her growled, startling her, and her face flamed. His back was to her. How in he hell could he know she was thinking inappropriate things about him?

Sense of smell. Oh yeah. Wow, this was mortifying. Sydney blushed even harder and was thankful when they reached the open air of the exercise yard. The moon was waxing. It would be full in just a couple of days. She wondered if she'd have to come out here with therians when that happened.

They'd all have to shift under the moon; they wouldn't be able to control or stop it. What if the wolf came after her then? Maybe if she talked to him. Maybe she could diffuse the situation somehow. Maybe when he was in wolf form he'd remember she was a friend and not food.

She followed him to the edge of the yard and tapped him on the shoulder. "Excuse me."

He rounded on her and growled. "WHAT?" That dangerous glow was in his eyes again.

"I-I'm Sydney."

"No," he said with a nasty sneer, "You are 5857B. And you'd better get used to it."

She couldn't believe she'd been attracted to him just minutes ago. More than just threatening and intimidating, out here where he could talk to her, he was just plain unpleasant.

"Well, sorry," she mumbled. "I just thought we didn't

have to hate each other." *Because I was hoping maybe then you wouldn't go psychotic on me later.*

Sydney took several steps back as he moved into her space.

"Let me be the one to educate you about things here. We are not going to be allies. You will *never* speak to me again. And if you have any sense in that stupid blonde head of yours, you won't attempt to call attention to your-self with any of the others, either. You are an abomina-tion. We smell your weakness, and everyone in this yard wants to rip you apart to undo the mistake your idiotic parents made. Stay the fuck away from all of us or learn the consequences of being what you are."

Sydney was stunned into silence. It wasn't as if she thought they were going to cuddle on the couch for movie night or anything, but she also hadn't expected such acidic words from someone who didn't even know her.

"GO!" he growled, pointing to the far end of the yard.

Noah watched Sydney scurry away from the other pris-oners. Good. Now if she could do that for just one more night because two nights from now, he was busting them out. She hadn't recognized him. But of course, she wouldn't. Her sense of smell wasn't as developed as his. And he'd changed so much from when they were kids. Then again, she had, too. She'd transformed from a child into a woman, and the looks a few of the others gave her as she passed, left no doubt.

He growled. He'd never get out of here with her. And he'd chew his own arm off before he left without her.

If he hadn't been sure before, he was sure now. Sydney was his true mate.

Just before he'd been kidnapped, Noah had asked his dad about mates. The words Cole had spoken would never leave him: "You can take anyone you want for a mate, but a true mate is determined by blood and destiny. She's out there somewhere. You'll be happier if you listen to the instinct and don't try to mark anyone but her."

It was a heavy conversation for an eight year old, but he'd taken it to heart.

He'd asked why his mom was a demon and not a werewolf like them. It had seemed strange, even though Noah had always thought it was the coolest thing in the world. Jane had become a demon when she'd died giving birth to him and had been stuck up in Heaven before the preternaturals had severed the link between that place and earth.

She'd had screens in her room in Heaven that allowed her to see what was happening with her family. She'd watched his father fall apart from losing her while Noah had been taken in by a panther therian and a witch. She'd begged to be returned to make things right. The catch was that she had to become a demon to do it. The mating bond with his father had been true, though, and they'd remained connected in the change, upgrading Noah's dad to an immortal in the process.

But before all that, his mom had started out human with a quirk. No one knew exactly how it had come to be, but she had some vampire blood in her veins. Since the first vampire had been created by an incubus and a werewolf, that blood made it possible for his mom to be Cole's true mate. His dad hadn't believed in true mates until he'd met her. After that, the overwhelming compulsion that overrode every other thought in his brain had been to protect her.

It was the same way Noah had always felt about Sydney. Even as a pup he'd never wanted to let her out of his sight, in case she needed him.

His mother had just enough blood that matched with werewolves to make being the alpha's true mate possible, but it wasn't as if werewolves were routinely taking mates with vampire blood. Still, Noah was as sure as his father had been. Sydney was his. And he *had* to get her out of here in one piece or he'd never recover from it.

Noah began his nightly run around the perimeter of the exercise yard. He couldn't afford to break routine when he was so close. They couldn't suspect anything or he'd lose the element of surprise and his only shot at getting out. In two nights he'd be strong enough, but he'd still have to do everything right. There was no margin for error. Especially not now.

As much as he'd wanted his freedom and to try to find his parents and pack, Noah had always accepted there was a chance he'd fail and either die or be punished severely for the infraction. It was an acceptable possibility a few nights ago, but not with Sydney in the mix. There was no scenario for defeat now.

He glanced her way every now and then when the progress in his perimeter lap wouldn't make it obvious he was watching her. She was doing as he'd suggested, staying far from everyone. Good. What he'd told her was true, except the parts about him wanting her away from him.

The others would smell and sense her weakness. It could initiate the predatory response. Why would the idiots running this place let her mix with the others? Unless that was their hope.

He'd initially been relieved they hadn't yet marked her with one of their terrible tattoos. But if they hadn't, it could only mean one thing. They didn't intend for her to live long enough to waste the ink.

4

Noah sat in the corner of his cell trying to ignore Sydney on the other side and running the plan for the following night in his head. It was hardest for him to ignore her when she slept. He didn't have to worry about her discovering things that could put her in danger. It was only the cameras he had to be concerned with. And sometimes they seemed barely real. It was harder to have the self control not to look at her when only hidden electronic eyes watched.

Noah felt the surge of power building for his birth moon, and for the first time he felt certain he could do this. It wasn't a pipe dream or a vain hope to keep him going.

If he could get her to go with him, he knew he could get them out of the building. The people in charge had gotten slack with the security, putting too much faith in how they had beaten the prisoners down over time. And they trusted too much in the canned raspberry-scented calm they sent in through the vents before they let them out for exercise each night.

The cells were secure. Noah had checked. Nobody was getting out of those. But during one of the brief windows when they were allowed outside them...

The powers that be had already slacked on the number of guards. They never needed them, so why keep them all on the payroll? Occasional fights broke out in the yard on full moons, so there would be higher security, but that still just meant one or two more guards.

There was a service elevator he'd glimpsed many times, and once five months ago, he'd had the rarest opportunity to go check it out when the only guard that day had gotten sick. The security in the elevator had major holes. He'd always been good with tech. He got that from his dad. He'd watched and absorbed all the ways the tech around him worked while he was still just a pup and not even in a human form yet. He was convinced he'd developed a photographic memory during his time in wolf form. It was a skill that served him well now.

As soon as he'd shifted to human for the first time, he'd started taking machines and computers apart and putting them back together using all the schematics his brain had been processing nearly from birth. The adults in the pack had been amazed, but machines had an internal logic if you listened to them and learned their language. He'd learned how to find bugs and holes in programs and fix them or exploit them from the moment he'd been gifted with opposable thumbs. Part of it might have been a native intelligence or something genetic from his father, but part of it had been the very nature of his earliest years.

From the moment Noah was born until the first time he shifted, he'd had nothing much to do but watch and absorb and wait. And now, inside this building for so many years waiting for his birth moon—the next time he would have the power to *act*—he'd once again had nothing to do but watch and learn and absorb and wait.

When he'd seen the problems with the computer in the service elevator, he prayed no one else knew about it. He doubted they did. They'd gotten too confident. Noah had quickly returned to his cell with the others after that to think about what he'd seen. He couldn't be sure what was outside the building but the idea of getting out of it ceased being an impossible dream after that.

Sydney stirred in her corner. He sensed the lab technician before he saw her. The glass door of the cell whooshed open and the woman moved into the room. Noah felt his muscles go rigid while his internal dialogue insisted that he had to remain cool and calm. He had to keep it together. He couldn't react. For Sydney's sake. Whatever they did, he couldn't react. If he reacted, they'd suspect something. It would risk her.

But the woman in the lab coat just wanted to chat. And he knew this one vaguely. Kristen. She was one of the less evil people in the facility. He hoped he was right about her.

Noah could hear their conversation through the glass, though it was muffled.

Kristen studied her clipboard. "We got the test results from the lab," she said.

"Oh?" Sydney said. She glanced his way then quickly away from him and back to the lab tech.

"You've stopped aging. We double-checked to make sure your aging hadn't just slowed, but no, you've stopped completely. Around six or seven years ago. Do you understand what this means?"

It meant they could keep her alive and keep her for centuries if they decided to. Though, the lack of tattoo had pointed to not letting her live long, maybe they'd change their mind on that score now that they knew she was conditionally immortal.

"It doesn't mean anything," Sydney said. "I'm not a *real* vampire. I'm too weak to survive for hundreds or thousands of years. It doesn't matter how my cells are aging or not aging."

"That sounds like denial to me," Kristen said. "Do you want to talk about it?"

Don't do it, Sydney. Don't trust her. This particular woman might not herself be the queen of evil, but she reported to someone who likely was. Noah held his breath, hoping Sydney wouldn't let them inside her thoughts.

As if he'd somehow managed to communicate that warning to her—or she was just smart—Sydney shook her head.

"No, that's okay. I'm just not as optimistic about it as you seem to be."

Kristen looked like she would argue, but two more lab techs were moving down the hallway toward

Sydney's cell. The door whooshed open again, and they tossed a badly beaten and bleeding human into the room.

Kristen seemed startled when the blood splattered her white shoes. "We observed you last night and noted that perhaps you might need to drink from a living source given your history. We know vampires can't stay as strong with bagged blood. Ordinarily we prefer that for our own safety, but you've been determined to be an exception to that rule."

Keep it together, Noah. Stay calm. Don't react. If he'd had any doubts that they now planned to keep her alive as long as possible, in the name of "science", those doubts had vanished. With her test results, they found her even more intriguing, which could only mean bad things.

The man groaned from the middle of the cell.

"Well," Kristen said, "I-I'll just leave you alone with your meal. We'll talk again in a few days, I'm sure." She patted Sydney awkwardly on the arm and then strode briskly out of the cell, sparing a glance at Noah while he tried to stay blank of discernible emotion.

"Don't worry, we weakened him so he can't harm you," one of the technicians said. Then both of them followed Kristen out of the cell, leaving Sydney alone with her beaten bloody dinner.

The man groaned again from the ground. "Syd?"

The bastard knew her? How could he know her?

"Jacob! Oh my God!" Sydney said. She approached him tentatively.

"Syd, I'm sorry. I'm so so sorry."

At first her face held sympathy and worry, perhaps curiosity over how this man she knew had come to be this way, but that initial instinct was replaced quickly with revulsion and a side of Sydney Noah hadn't yet seen.

"Oh, I bet you're sorry, *now*. Now that your own plots and schemes have come back to bite you. You betrayed me! You sold me to them for a piece of paper with an address on it. What was the problem? Parents not home?"

"T-there was nothing there. It was a factory. They just wanted you, and they thought they'd take me as unpaid labor. They never knew anything about my family. Or if they did, they never planned to tell me."

Noah watched as she paced in her cell and circled Jacob a few times, looking for the first time like the predator she was supposed to be if she hadn't been born with only human strength.

"So I'm right. If you'd found them and had a happy reunion you wouldn't have thought about me ever again."

"Syd, that's not true. You know it's not. I like you. I told you I've always liked you."

"I hate to think about what you'd do to somebody you didn't like. You piece of shit." She kicked him in the thigh, barely budging him, but being already injured, he still winced.

Jacob struggled to sit and pulled off his ripped and blood-covered shirt. And there it was, the slightest shift in Sydney's scent, in her reaction to him. Noah knew without any doubt that they had been lovers. They had history.

Noah looked away. If he kept looking at the human, he'd shift and lose his shit. Jacob had two very big marks against him. He'd betrayed Sydney and brought her to this place, and he'd slept with her. The first thing made Noah so livid he had to take long, deep breaths to stay calm.

Don't react. Don't react. Don't react. They'll know if you react.

The second thing merely annoyed him. But it annoyed him pretty strongly. Of course, it was irrational to be upset about anything Sydney had done with someone else before him. Noah didn't even know the circumstances of their encounters. Had he expected her to remain some pure virgin for him? That would be insane. Of course he didn't expect that, especially not when he hadn't even been there for her.

He'd just never thought he'd have to look at the bastard or bastards she'd been with.

And it wasn't as if Sydney knew he was still alive. She probably had no idea who she was to him. Even without Jacob, Noah might have his work cut out for him trying to convince her that she could be happy with the jerk who'd yelled at her in the exercise yard. There was some big trust-building ahead of them. Jacob was the least of his problems.

"Syd you need to feed," Jacob said moving closer to her.

Her lip curled in disgust. "From you? Are you kidding me? As if I would *ever* want to put my fangs inside of you again. Especially after you electrocuted me with that black box thing!"

He'd *electrocuted* her? Noah was starting to suspect he was being baited here. There was just too much for him to react to. He'd reacted too emotionally the first time he'd seen her. Maybe they suspected it was something more than the hate he was trying to play off now. Was he being too paranoid? Maybe, but was there any level of paranoid that was too paranoid given his current living conditions and the stakes involved in getting him and Sydney safely to tomorrow night when he might be strong enough to protect her?

The cheery robotic voice filled Sydney's cell. "We're going to have to insist that you feed. You need to keep your strength up."

"This place is creepy as hell," Jacob said.

"Yeah, thanks for that. I don't even have anyone to talk to here. You see that guy over there?" She pointed at Noah and he let his eyes glow and fangs come out because it seemed to go with the "look how much I hate this girl" vibe he was trying to throw out.

Jacob turned and looked at him, then scrambled back closer to her. *Yeah, you better run you little shit.*

"That psycho already threatened me in the yard and basically told me I can't talk to anybody here or they might kill me. So not only am I a prisoner *again,* now, I don't even have any friends or people who love me!"

Don't be so sure about that.

"And I just found out I don't age, so who knows what that means?"

"Come on, Syd. You'll feel better when you've had some blood."

When her fangs came out, Noah found himself torn between jealousy and hoping she'd lose control and drain the guy. Sydney glared pointedly at Noah, and he looked away. She didn't like anybody watching her. Fine. He didn't particularly want to watch her suck neck in front of him, anyway.

He tried not to imagine it was him she was drinking and not that stupid boy. The human was close to their age, but no *man* would throw someone vulnerable under the bus like he had Sydney. That was what a boy did.

Several minutes passed while Noah watched as inconspicuously as possible with his peripheral vision. He could hear her and smell her, and if nothing else, he would have known she'd finished when she pushed Jacob away with some effort. He fell with a dull thud on the thick, shatterproof glass.

The voice spoke again in Sydney's cell. "Please *finish* your dinner."

Sydney seemed horrified by the suggestion. Even after everything this man had done to her, she couldn't bring herself to kill him. It would have been an easy choice for Noah. He would have killed the fucker in a heartbeat, but she wasn't like that. Even from his childhood memories of her, she was too sensitive. She'd see it as cold-blooded murder.

Noah thought she would fight to defend herself from a threat. She might kill in self-defense or accidentally, but he couldn't see her taking a life for revenge or just for the thrill of the kill.

"There are starving vampires in the world," the robotic voice reasoned. "And here you are leaving food on your plate. I'm sorry, but we can't allow that."

The human was distressed, his weakening heartbeat speeding at the threat. He might just give out from fear. It would spare Sydney the task of finishing him.

Her face was a solid, stubborn wall. She wasn't going to do it. Noah wanted to shake her. She didn't yet understand that you didn't say no here. To anything.

Lasers of UV light blasted from the corners of her cell. The smoke rose off her flesh and she let out a shriek that chilled his blood.

Don't react. Don't react. You can't react. Keep it together. One more day, Noah.

He turned away, feigning boredom, because no matter how much he knew he couldn't react if he wanted the opportunity to get her out of here, he knew he couldn't remain stoic if he had to watch this. She just had to survive until tomorrow night.

Finish him, Noah pleaded in his mind, as if he could send her a mental message and have it take hold.

"Oh, no," the robotic voice said, sounding not at all concerned. "It doesn't look like you're healing. You should finish your dinner."

Noah sneaked a brief glance. It was true. She wasn't healing. There were several round burn marks on her from the lasers. She barely had the strength to crawl to Jacob.

"No, Syd, don't do it!" her prey said.

As if her refusal would actually spare the human's life. Whatever he'd done to piss them off, they didn't forgive easily and he wasn't getting out of here alive whatever Sydney did or didn't do. Finally, she took his arm and she drank until his heart stopped. Then she collapsed into sobbing fits over the body.

"Take him away!" she screamed. "Take him away!"

The door to Noah's cell slid open and the big plate of raw meat was shoved in. He glanced again at Sydney. If he ate the meat he'd fall asleep. What if they hurt her while he was out? What if they hurt her more while he was awake and he reacted and she lost her one chance to get out of here? He had to maintain the routine.

He shifted into his wolf form and ate.

The dream world came into focus sharper and more real than Noah's waking world. The memories he couldn't access in his waking hours came forth bright and crisp. He was about seven. It had been dark out for a while now, and Sydney was supposed to come over later. He couldn't wait to see her.

But his dad and her dad were outside yelling at each other.

"Noah is strong," Anthony said. "And he's her friend. His blood might make her stronger. The human blood is barely keeping her going, and I can't stand to see her cry when she accidentally kills one of them. She's just a kid. She's not like me."

"Something we can all be grateful for," Cole said.

"So, you'll ask Noah?"

His dad growled. "Never! I don't care if you and I have worked together a few times over the years. Those kids have an unnatural attachment to one another, and I should have put a stop to it a long time ago. If you think I would let some vampire sink her dirty fangs into my kid..."

Noah jumped at the sound of flesh hitting flesh and then growled when he realized the vampire king had just hit his dad. Cole growled back, and another punch was landed. This time it was Anthony who let out the groan of pain.

"Don't you bring that little freak near my son ever again, do you hear me?" Cole said. "In fact, why don't you keep your vampires at the compound, and I'll keep my wolves at the hive? You stay on that side of town. I'll stay on this one."

Noah gasped. How could his dad call Sydney a name like that? She was the nicest person he knew, and the only kid near his age that he didn't have to try to impress. She didn't care that he was the alpha's son.

After the vampire king left, Noah moved out into the open. "Dad?"

Cole growled and spun around. "How much of that did you hear?"

He shrugged. How could he know how much he'd heard or when they'd started arguing? "Is Sydney sick? If she needs blood, she can have some of mine to get better."

"Absolutely not. I'm sorry, but you can't play with her anymore. We don't make friends with vampires. I should have stopped it when it first started, but your mom is friends with Charlee, and it just seemed easier to let it go."

Was mom not allowed to see Charlee now? He

couldn't imagine his dad had any power to stop a demon from going wherever she wanted.

Noah felt the glow come to his eyes. "That is *bullshit*! You can't stop me from seeing her!"

Cole's nostrils flared. "Where did you learn that word?"

There was a saying that little wolves had big ears, and the pack hadn't been editing their vocabulary around him recently.

Noah shrugged again and mumbled, "You can't stop me from seeing her."

The alpha's eyes narrowed. "I'm the alpha. I can make anybody stop seeing anybody."

But even at seven, Noah knew that to some degree his dad was all talk. After all, he wouldn't throw his own son out of the pack. Not over something like this. And especially not when he was still a pup, despite all his big talk.

He didn't see Sydney again after that. He still thought about her and missed her. He wondered if she thought about him and missed him. As soon as he was old enough and strong enough, he would go find her. But that never happened because the following year he was kidnapped.

As he was taken away by the magic users, he thought, *Bet you wish you'd just let me hang out with Sydney now, instead of getting too close to the pack kids.*

If he'd been allowed to see her, he wouldn't have been playing chicken with the boundaries because he wouldn't have cared what the other pack kids thought. He wouldn't have done something that might have encouraged Sydney to join in and put her in danger.

SYDNEY SAT in her cell staring at the spot where Jacob had been. They hadn't even properly cleaned the cube. She could still smell him in there. A few careless drops of blood remained as evidence of what she'd done the day before.

What they made you do.

Not long before, she'd been plotting to kill him. But it had been different. It had been an escape plan to save her life. But didn't doing what they said save her life? When she'd killed him and then watched the guy in the cube beside her shift nonchalantly into his wolf form and eat like nothing had happened, she knew she was truly friendless in here.

She'd been given bagged blood this evening. It didn't restore her energy but at least she wasn't killing someone today. It was something. If they weren't going to let her feed from a human without demanding she finish him, this was better.

Sydney studied the burn marks. Several ran up and down her arms. In the reflective glass she could see one on her cheek. Another had hit the side of her neck. A normal vampire would have healed instantly unless he'd been weakened and starved. Not Sydney. It hadn't even started to heal a day later. These marks would scar.

She felt the tears start up again. The wolf stirred in the corner of his cell. He'd had his drugged meat a few hours ago, and the sleep was wearing off. He shifted back to his human form and turned away from her to put on the new clothes they'd brought him. Sydney got to go for a shower right after waking up. She assumed the wolf went in the mornings while she was dead for the day.

She couldn't even bring herself to find him attractive anymore. Physically he was still as perfect as ever, but when he'd nearly made her cry in the exercise yard it had cured her of any fleeting crush. What was it with her and wolves? When she was a kid she used to spend every moment until she had to go to sleep with Noah.

Noah. Now the tears did fall. It wasn't as if she thought about him all the time anymore, but lately, seeing the wolf in the next cube every day was too hard. It brought back too many memories. She hadn't been allowed to play with him for a while before he disappeared. She didn't know why her father and Noah's dad had started their feud, but the result was that they couldn't play together anymore.

She'd cried in her room for weeks after that, but it was nothing compared to the night she'd overheard that he'd gone missing. It wasn't until that night that she'd known she'd never see him again. She'd refused to leave her room for a month after that.

The wolf in the cube next to hers glared at her, then stared expectantly at the door waiting for exercise time. He seemed extra amped up tonight. It had to be the moon. She feared she wouldn't survive out there with the moon full and everyone shifting. There were only a couple of other vampires in this group, and they were unlikely to protect her from any threats out there. They'd probably been waiting for an excuse to join in on the killing.

"Number 5857B, Please prepare to exit your cell for

daily exercise," the happy robot voice said. Sydney knew some of the messages were pre-recorded, but sometimes when the voice spoke it still sounded robotic, but sentient. She wondered if it was artificial intelligence or if someone typed into the machine what it should say.

It wasn't as if she exercised out there. She mainly just tried to stay out of everyone else's way until it was time to come back inside. The glass door slid open.

"Please follow the glowing arrows to the exercise yard, and remember to play nice with your friends."

She was pushed aside by several therians racing to get outside under the full moon, so she was the last out. She missed the frenzied shifting. By the time she reached the yard it was like a zoo. Cheetahs, panthers, wolves, bears. There wasn't yard big enough for the insanity.

Sydney looked up. The moon was red. Aunt Greta once told her about the blood moon and how powerfully strong it was for therians. Great. Just what she didn't need.

She tried to disappear next to a nearby wall as the shapeshifters ran and started fights and burned excess energy under the moon. A wolf leaped at her, but a second wolf body slammed him away from her and started to snarl and snap at him. The wolf that had come at her was bleeding now and slunk off to lick his wounds.

The smell of therian blood got to the other two vampires and they joined in the fray to try to get a taste of the blood being spilled left and right in the fighting. The blood was getting to Sydney, too, but she knew if she listened to that urge she wouldn't come out of it alive. The other vampires could hold their own out there.

The robotic voice chirped happily over the loud speakers. "I think that's enough excitement for today, please make your way back to the building."

It was extremely short for an exercise period, and Sydney knew why. The blood moon had been more than they'd anticipated. There were more guards than last night, but it still wasn't enough to contain it all.

As they moved back inside away from the influence of the moon, therians began shifting back to their human forms, and Sydney found herself surrounded by a bunch of naked people who still seemed way too keyed up to be in an enclosed space with. A hand latched onto her arm.

She turned to find a very naked 5856 looking at her with an intensity that unnerved her.

"We have to get out of here, Sydney." He'd used her name. He'd *remembered* her name. Why had he just used her name? The other night he'd made it perfectly clear that she was an identifying number—a cog in the machine—and nothing more.

He dragged her down a secondary hallway, not the one with the arrows, another, darker hallway with more glass cubes. But this area wasn't used; the lights were out. Sydney could barely see here, but she knew the wolf could see just fine in the dark. His eyes were glowing an eerie yellow.

All kinds of fucked-up thoughts went through her head. She tried to pull free, and then a guard appeared and helped her get out of his grasp, but the wolf let out a savage growl and snapped the guard's neck. 5856 dragged Sydney down a couple more side hallways. One of them was dimly lit with flickering lights that hissed. They ran right into the lady in the lab coat who'd given Sydney her test results. The wolf grabbed her like he might kill her too, but then he let her go.

"Don't make me regret it, Kristen."

She shook her head and ran in the opposite direction.

At the end of the hallway was a steel elevator.

"Thumbprint required for entry," a recorded voice said out of the box next to the elevator.

He shifted partially and used his claw to rip open the box. He tore out a few wires and pressed a bunch of buttons on the keypad in quick succession.

"Thank you," the computer said as the doors slid open.

"Come on," he snarled, dragging her into the enclosed space with him.

Sydney moved into the back corner of the elevator as if she could go invisible. He was obviously attempting to break out of here, and he'd get her killed doing it. Why had he brought her with him? Was she a hostage?

The elevator went down what felt like thousands of floors but was probably only about thirty-five. The wolf was still naked, his clothing lying somewhere out in the exercise yard with all the others. She shrank back when he turned to her.

"I don't know the whole layout of this place, but my guess is the security bug is throughout the building. At least I hope it is if we need to go through anymore thumbprint scanners. When we get outside, I'll shift again under the moon. I can't stop it. Whatever you do, follow me, and when we get to the edge of the city, run for the desert and do not stop. I'll be right behind you."

"Why—"

But the door opened on the ground level, and he grabbed her arm again.

The happy robotic voice said, "5856 and 5857B are out of their rooms, please stop them and bring them to the courtesy desk if you see them. Thank you."

Sydney froze in the face of the melee. There were too many people in lab coats running toward them. Some had weapons. The wolf's eyes darted around as if he were doing math equations in his head, then he grabbed her and tossed her in a big laundry bin nearby. She landed on a soft pile of freshly laundered white clothes and peeked out to see him shift again. He moved faster than she could track, dodging bursts of light that came out of the weapons. He ripped out throat after throat until dead bodies covered the floor with little room to walk.

"Unit B, please report to the lobby," the voice said. Sydney wasn't sure if she imagined the voice sounding somehow less cheerful and upbeat this time.

The wolf shifted back to his human form, ran for her and lifted her out of the bin. He carried her, running to the doors. "Remember what I said."

Outside he set her down and immediately shifted, then he began to run. Sydney ran behind him. She didn't have the kind of stamina he did, and she'd had bagged blood. She was going to lose him, but she pushed and ran even though her lungs burned, because if she didn't they'd kill her tonight. There was no way they'd bother with her any further when she'd proven to be so much trouble. She'd seen action movies, ancient and outdated though they were.

The lights of the city were practically blinding. Loud-speakers were everywhere and the same cheery robotic voice she'd heard every day inside the building was speaking, only this speech was intended for a very different audience.

"Everyone likes a good citizen. If you see something strange, please report it to one of the officers so that we can help keep everyone safe. Please stay far away from the perimeter. We can't protect you out there. There is no need to fear the wilderness. Only bad people go there. You're a good person. You would never do anything wrong."

Sydney saw the perimeter and ran. There was a giant red sign that read *Turn back, wilderness less than 500 feet.* She ran straight for it, and a few seconds later crossed into the open space outside the boundary of the city. She turned back to see the wolf bounce off an invisible barrier. Why had she gone through but he bounced off?

Because you're not a real vampire.

Except this time, for once, it might have saved her life. The wolf began to dig, and she kept running.

When she reached the desert, she stopped short at the sight of a wall of vampires and werewolves all in their wolf form. The wolves growled.

"Pretty thing all alone outside the city," one of the vampires said leaving the line of them to approach her.

When he got closer, he sniffed the air, and his eyes narrowed. "You aren't a human." He grabbed her by the shoulders as if to shake her. "What are you," he demanded.

A wolf jumped up and bit him on the arm, and the vampire let go of her. It wasn't one of the wolves from the group. It was her cell neighbor. He put himself between her and the others and growled something to the other wolves. They growled back. And Sydney might be going crazy, but it seemed like they were actually talking to each other instead of just making random angry sounds.

One of the wolves struggled to reclaim a human form. It was a female wolf. She had a black snake tattoo that wrapped around her upper arm, slithering all the way down her forearm. Not that the smirking vampires were looking at her tattoo. She was attractive and naked, and occasionally vampires could be pigs.

The woman rolled her eyes. "Shut up." She turned to Sydney. "Sydney?"

"Umm, yes?" Sydney wasn't a hundred percent sure she wasn't in her cube dreaming all this.

"You guys come with me. I'm going to take you some place safe. You can stay with my pack."

"We aren't just letting them go," the vampire that had grabbed Sydney said as if he were upset his only entertainment of the night was being taken from him. "That *thing* shouldn't even be alive."

Her wolf—because it was all Sydney could think of him as, now that there were about twenty of them all standing around snarling—growled at the vampire. But then a second vampire said, "Shut up, guys. There's a LOT of dinner coming right for us."

The vampires lost interest in them as unit B showed up. They and the remaining wolves converged on the humans as the female wolf shifted to lead Sydney and the guy who'd inexplicably saved her life, to the den.

5

The makeshift den was only about five miles outside the city's perimeter, but Sydney felt like she might drop at any moment. The sun would be up in a few hours, and she couldn't remember ever feeling this exhausted.

The den was an old train station that looked to have been converted into a hotel and restaurant before it became a werewolf den. A large connected building rose behind the main lobby that no doubt had accommodated human guests at one point. When they got through the first set of doors into what had once been the station, the two wolves shifted back, neither of them concerned with their nudity.

"This guy is staying with us while he forms a plan to get his girl back to their place. I'm sorry, what was your name?"

Sydney hadn't cared what the surly werewolf's name was a few hours ago. She'd only hoped she never had to interact with him again. But now it was getting a little weird. She couldn't call him "5856" or "Hey you". And if she called him "her wolf" in front of anybody else for lack of a better naming convention, she might just go greet the sun in her embarrassment. Better to roast to death than to have to suffer through his nasty sneer again.

Before mystery wolf could reply, several other people —werewolves—filed into the main lobby. "What the hell is *that*?" one of the males asked, pointing at her.

When she'd spent all her time in the compound, she'd known she was weird, but it hadn't been driven home just *how* weird, until everyone else in the outside world seemed able to pick up on it instantly. And whatever they were picking up on, they didn't like.

The woman who'd brought them caught a pair of pants and top mid-air when they were tossed at her and began to dress. "They are our guests until tomorrow night. They need some place safe for when the sun comes up."

"Oh, no," the guy said. "*That* is not staying here."

Her wolf, now in his human form and very very naked, growled and moved into the other wolf's space. "She is mine. She goes where I go."

"Oh yeah?"

The female wolf stepped between the posturing males. "Cool it, Rafe. This one is strong. You don't want to challenge him."

Was she their leader? Sydney wasn't sure. Maybe she was part of an alpha pair, but she was obviously strong to be able to reclaim her human form under a blood moon.

A full moon by itself would have been impressive enough.

"If she's *his* then why hasn't he marked her?"

The sound of flesh hitting flesh echoed off the walls of the old train station lobby as she slapped him. "That's enough, Rafe. I said they stay. Unless you want to challenge me?"

He dropped to one knee and offered his throat. "No, Ma'am."

Shit, she *was* the leader.

"That's better."

Sydney's wolf spoke up, then. "Can I borrow some clothes, and I'd like some privacy. I haven't had a chance to explain things to her. I just found her."

"Of course. We have a few rooms built against the original structure that don't have windows. That would be safest."

"Thanks."

The look she gave him made Sydney wonder if the alpha wanted Noah leading beside her, but the female wolf seemed to shake herself out of it. "No problem." She barely spared a glance to Sydney.

A pair of sweatpants and a T-shirt sailed through the air, and he snatched the clothing and put it on.

When they reached the windowless room, the alpha said, "I'm Shira, by the way. You never told me your name."

Was she flirting with him?

"Later," he said. "I need to talk with her first."

Her smile was tight. "Sure, no problem."

When she'd disappeared down the hallway he shut and locked the door, then shoved a chair under it.

Sydney took a step back. "Ummm." He'd better start explaining something fast.

He put his hands in the air. "Relax. Without a window, we don't have an alternate exit. I need a warning if they decide to come in guns blazing. I think she's only helping us because she didn't want me to challenge her for her pack. I have no interest in her pack. I just want to go home."

"I'm sorry, but who the hell *are* you? And why did you take me out of there? You made it pretty clear you hated me. I can't figure out why you'd bust me out with you if you find my very existence so vile."

He kept staring at her mouth. She didn't like the way he kept staring at her mouth. Or maybe she did. No she didn't. She didn't know. If he turned out to be only moderately crazy, maybe she did.

"I'm Sorry. Everything I said to you, everything you think you saw was only to protect you. There was surveillance everywhere, and I couldn't risk them thinking I cared what happened to you. I had to wait on the moon. When everything started happening, there wasn't time to explain, and then once we were here, I preferred privacy to tell you."

"Tell me what?"

"Sydney, do you not remember me at all?" He looked almost hurt.

She shook her head slowly, but a hope started to bloom in her chest. She wouldn't let the name form in her mind. If she thought it and then it wasn't true... And it couldn't be true, anyway. He couldn't have survived this long.

"You *do* remember."

"I don't know what you're talking about."

"Noah. I'm Noah."

Before she'd thought she might drop from exhaustion, but now she hurled herself into his arms with renewed energy. "Noah?" She looked hard into his eyes, the planes of his face, his smile, his hair. He was only a boy the last time she'd seen him, but he looked a bit like his dad now that she thought about it.

Why hadn't she realized that before? Maybe because he'd looked so angry all the time.

"Noah? It's really you? We thought you were dead!"

He held her while she cried. She couldn't believe it had been him in the cube next to hers.

"It's my twenty-eighth birth moon. I was planning to break out tonight. I've been planning it for months. I didn't know it would be a blood moon, though. When it was, it was just that much luckier. I was afraid I wasn't going to be able to get you out of there. I couldn't take any chances that they might separate you into another group before it was time. I almost lost my mind when they burned you, but I couldn't let it show."

Noah. She'd spent years trying to push the memory of him into the background of her mind. She'd spent an equal amount of time pretending that not being able to feel love for Jacob before had nothing to do with her little girl crush on the werewolf.

"Sydney, you're my mate."

She searched his face. "What do you mean, mate?

You mean... like a friend?" Was this the, *I like you but not that way,* speech—just in case she was getting ideas in her head after his big "she's mine" thing out in the train lobby?

Then his impossibly warm lips were moving over hers, his large hands tangled in her hair. Her brain decided at that point to tell her about forty times that Noah was kissing her, just in case she was having a black-out/out-of-body experience combo and had missed the memo.

After a couple of minutes, she pulled away first. "So... n-not a friend?"

He smirked. "Not a friend."

Noah didn't ask how she felt about it. He didn't need to. She was smiling so hard her face hurt.

Then he let out an angry growl. He turned her face toward the light. "Look at what those bastards did to you. It still hasn't healed. I need you to feed from me."

It wasn't that she didn't want to. The idea of drinking from Noah was about the best menu offer she could ever remember receiving. It was just that she wasn't sure if she was quite ready to move things that fast. If she fed on him she wasn't sure if she'd be able to keep her clothes on, and what if he was wrong? What if she wasn't his true mate?

What if he hooked up with that alpha bitch and realized he'd just missed Sydney because she'd been familiar and had reminded him of home?

He ran his fingers through her hair. "What is it, Sydney?" He'd never called her Syd. Even when they were kids.

"How do you *know* I'm her? I mean you were locked up in that horrible place for so long. It's only natural that someone from your past might make you feel a certain way and..."

"Sydney, no. It's you. Don't you remember how we were when we were kids? I guarded you half the time when you slept. For hours. That's not normal. And I would have watched over you every day if the adults had let me. I knew when we were kids, I just couldn't articulate it. But I'm not a kid anymore. I know you're my true mate."

"My father will never allow us..."

Noah snorted. "Anthony has no say in this. You're an adult. It only matters what *you* want."

"Oh, so if I said, 'You're a nice guy, Noah, but I just like you as a friend,' that would be it?"

He rolled his eyes. "You feel it, too. Maybe not as strong because you're not a wolf, but you know it's always been you and me."

He pulled her back into his arms and gently pressed her face against his neck. Her fangs obligingly came out.

"Feed," he whispered. "And just a friendly warning... you can do whatever you want, but if clothes come off, I will mark you, so be sure you're ready to commit to me before you try to seduce me."

His voice rumbled against her when he spoke.

She sank her fangs into his throat in response because she didn't trust her voice, and she might say something stupid enough for him to reconsider this true mate business.

He was her favorite flavor, uncomplicated desire. It

was an emotional bouquet that she'd felt strange savoring before because it had always come from someone she didn't want in equal measure. It was like reading the diary of someone who had a crush on her. It had felt dirty and like violating someone's privacy. But Noah had already let her in.

It was the taste of his blood that took away her doubts. At least in his own mind, he was completely sure she was his mate. And for now, that had to be enough. It wasn't as if there was a way one could prove a true mate. There was no lab test that could be done. There was no potion they could drink that would reveal all. You just had to take the leap and trust it.

The flavor was intoxicating, but the strength of the blood was hard to take. She only drank a little before pulling away.

"You need more," he said gently, to get her to keep feeding. "I don't mind." He took her hand and pressed it against the front of his pants. "I like it."

If any other guy had done something like that, she would have had a panic attack and fantasized about drop kicking him, but as far as she was concerned, Noah could put her hand anywhere he liked.

"Just let me get used to it," she said. "I've only drank regular humans before." It was like going from watered down wine to 100-proof whiskey. Or like trying to consume an entire chocolate cake in one go.

He chuckled. "You do wonderful things for my ego, Sydney."

She looked down at her arm. The burn marks from the UV laser were gone.

6

Noah still couldn't believe they'd made it out, that she was in his arms now, and that she seemed on board with the mate thing. He would have understood if she'd argued more. Of if she hadn't seemed as into it. If it took her feelings a while to catch up to what his blood had always known, it was the price he would have gladly paid. He would have given her time, but the way it was going, he may have her marked before the sun came up.

That would be his preference given how defenseless she'd be during the day. But he'd guard her from the moment she fell dead for the day until she woke again. She made another effort at drinking from him, taking more this time.

He shivered when her tongue ran over his neck to lap up the drops that had spilled. He felt himself heal as she pulled away and got a funny look on her face.

"That doesn't usually happen," she said.

"What doesn't?"

"T-the healing. I can't heal my umm... meals... after biting like other vampires can."

It was so adorable the way she struggled for a word as if he didn't understand she was using him as a food source.

Noah kissed her on the cheek. "That was my healing. I heal fast." Faster now that he'd come into his full powers.

"Oh."

He examined the places where she'd been burned again. It was fresh, clean skin, no scars, no evidence it had ever happened. Good.

Sydney looked down at her arms where the marks had been. "I didn't think they would heal at all. Usually if I don't feed right after an incident, I can't heal properly. It's part of why my dad has been so protective."

She bent her arm. "Like this place on my elbow..."

"What place on your elbow?"

She twisted to look. "Maybe it's the other one. It was a long time ago." She checked the other one. "It's gone."

Noah smiled. They should have let her feed from him when they were kids. Who cared what anybody thought? It would have made her healthy and strong. It still might.

She spent the next five minutes twisting and turning, checking for all the scars that had piled up in her existence. "They're all gone. All of them."

"I need to go talk to the pack alpha. I'll be back here before the sun comes up, but lock the door behind me and block it with the chair. Don't open it for anyone but me. As soon as the sun sets again, we'll leave."

She nodded, a serious expression on her face. He was glad she seemed to grasp the danger of being in another pack's den. But then Sydney's life had probably been nothing but caution.

When he'd closed the door behind him, he waited to hear the deadbolt snap into place and the sound of the chair jamming against the door handle, then he made his way down the elevator and back into the main lobby.

In the corner was a baby grand piano that had obviously been there when the place was a hotel. To one side was a bar that also looked like it had been there for a while. The bar had been brought back into service, and several of the wolves were in there, tossing back a few. Others sprawled on old sofas and chairs with the stuffing coming out while metal played over the sound system. More than half of them were lying around sans clothing because it was the full moon. They would shift and hunt or run then come back for a while and drink.

It looked like a Bacchanalia down here, and Noah was glad he'd left Sydney in the room. He smelled sex on the air. He worried he wouldn't have been able to keep Sydney safe in this and was thankful when they'd arrived that most of the wolves were out on their initial full moon run or hadn't been outside yet.

Piles of clothing littered the floor. Most of the wolves probably wouldn't dig through the pile to find their clothes until the next morning.

The main doors were constantly opening and shutting as wolves shifted and ran out. A few ran back in, shifted back, and dropped onto one of many sofas, goofy grins on their faces. The blood moon was making everyone high, and the alcohol wasn't helping. There would be two more nights of this insanity before the moon began to wane. He had to get Sydney out of here before it got too crazy. Tomorrow night would be even worse.

Eyes followed him as he moved through the lobby and toward the bar. They sensed power, and a couple of them seemed ready to throw their fealty at him. It was natural for werewolves. Most weren't comfortable being outside a strongly organized social order, and most weren't driven to lead. They wanted to know who to follow, who to answer to, and who would keep them safe. When a stronger wolf came into a pack, there was always a risk that wolf could take over as alpha.

If Noah wanted to take this pack and run it, he could. Easily. He'd have to mark Sydney first, so she'd be safe. The idea of running a pack appealed to him on a deep instinctual level, but he had to get back to his family.

He wasn't sure if he could go back and be a member of his dad's pack and not feel that hot feeling under his skin that recoiled at not having his own group to run, but he needed to see them and spend time with them. Maybe a lot of time.

He needed to learn how to re-integrate with normal life on the outside. No matter his strength or instincts, he knew he wasn't fit to lead, not after being a caged animal for so many long years. Even just being around this many other werewolves without a structured routine and cells to divide them, made him feel unhinged.

Noah wouldn't show Sydney that side of him. He couldn't. She had to feel safe and know she was protected. She didn't need to have to deal with his mental issues on top of everything else. He'd have to work it out privately for himself. He'd figure out what normal was. He'd blend. It would be fine. But right now being anybody's alpha was the last thing he needed in his life, no matter how many heads seemed to incline the most imperceptible amount when he neared.

Their current alpha sensed it, too, and she was in panic mode. As he moved into the bar, the metal from the lobby faded to make room for smooth jazz, but the two still met at the door and clashed liked fighting siblings.

The wolf behind the bar put a glass in front of him. "What'll you have?"

Noah wasn't sure how things worked here. Did they use some form of currency? Was it all on the house because it was pack? He wasn't sure if he was being treated as a guest or a patron. He held up a hand. "I'm fine."

He'd never had alcohol, but they didn't need to know that. They didn't need to know he'd never drank, never hunted like a real wolf, never had sex even. If they knew any of that, the sycophants among them would go back to their current leader and fawn over her.

"You're our guest. Try this."

Noah watched an amber liquid being poured into a small glass. He caught another wolf tossing back a similar drink in one gulp. The other wolf slammed his hand on the bar and let out a howl. "That's harsh, Rafe. Damn. Did you mix it with battery acid this time?"

The wolf behind the bar chuckled.

Oh great. Noah knew this. He was being tested. It was something he understood. Being watched and studied and tested and measured was familiar. He knew how this worked.

His eyes never left Rafe's, not even to look at the glass, as he picked it up and drank it down. Holy shit. What the fuck was that? He covered an impending cough with a growl and said. "Another."

Respect. He passed.

"Nobody can take two shots of Rafe's home brew whiskey. Trust me on this one," the wolf Noah had watched pound one back said.

"I'm sure I can handle it," Noah said.

He tossed the second one back and resisted the urge to melt into hysterics as the alcohol burned down his throat.

He stood from the bar and moved to the back of the lounge and sat in an old overstuffed chair in a corner so he could see the doorway and anyone approaching him. Thankfully no one was. He recalled how his dad had been with the pack. When Cole had been distant, they seemed to hang on to every word he said more.

They interpreted distance and silence as strength and power. But Noah wasn't trying to give off any of that, he just couldn't handle that many people crammed around him. The extent of how different he was from the other wolves was only just now becoming clear.

When he'd been imprisoned, the canned mechanical

voice had kept order. He didn't know how the world worked out here, how anything worked without a small glass cell to go back to and spend most of his time in. He'd been surrounded by silence for so long that any amount of raucous noise made him want to crawl under a table and hide, but if he showed that kind of weakness, they'd join together and attack, and soon after they took him out, Sydney would be at their mercy.

He couldn't let that happen, so he had to fake it. All they knew was that he'd escaped from the city. They had no way to know how long he'd been in there. They couldn't know that all he knew about how packs worked and how life worked was from fragmented childhood memories, instinct, and the tiny bits of conversation he'd picked up over the years in the yard from his runs.

Many of his fellow prisoners had been taken as adults. They had entire histories to reference back to. He'd listened to them talk and had practiced sounding like them because if he didn't, he'd known when he broke out of there, he'd sound like some stiff robot and would never be able to successfully blend into life anywhere.

Noah thought back to the escape. In so many ways they'd been lucky. He'd been terrified they wouldn't make it past the service elevator. And then what would happen to Sydney? He'd long ago stopped caring what happened to him. If his escape wasn't successful, he'd be happiest dead, but Sydney had given him the will to believe failure wasn't an option. Failing himself was nothing, but if he failed her...

He'd never killed anyone before. When the guard

had grabbed Sydney and took advantage of Noah's distraction to jerk her free of him, he'd reacted on instinct. And in the lobby, he'd known it was them or Sydney. As he'd scooped her out of the laundry bin and run for the door, he'd glanced back at the macabre tableau he'd created with fangs and clawed hands. Why didn't he feel anything?

Shouldn't he have felt guilt, remorse, horror? Something? But he was blank. He wasn't even sure what he was supposed to feel about it. But if he could just flip like that, fly into a rage and take dozens of people out, was Sydney safe with him?

He'd become too anti-social locked away from the world, isolated even from his fellow prisoners. It was too many years without any socialization. The orders and routines had substituted for pack hierarchy, and for a while it had fooled some part of his brain into going along with it.

He'd spent years repressing everything inside him that screamed to fight, because he'd known it was the wrong time to fight. He would only lose, and he shouldn't start a fight he couldn't win. But tonight, all the pent up aggression and rebellion rose up out of him with the power of the moon, and he'd reacted. It was as if an invisible trigger had been pulled. He'd gone from mild-mannered, quiet Noah, to crazy-killing-machine Noah in an eye-blink.

He looked up to find the alpha striding toward him. For whatever reason, she was running this pack alone, and he smelled the fear on her. If he could smell it, just having met her, he knew her pack could smell it. He knew she feared losing her wolves to him, but at this point, she may as well fear losing it to any one of the werewolves in the bar. If there was one thing he remembered from his dad, it was that the alpha couldn't show fear to anyone.

Even if no one was waiting in the wings to take over, it de-stabilized the pack and introduced petty squabbling among the other wolves, testing boundaries, trying to find a barrier they would bounce off of so they could feel safe and cohesive again.

Shira scanned the room. Noah felt a wall go up around her as she pushed the fear down and tried to cover it. But she wasn't nearly the expert at covering emotion that Noah had become, and everyone had already seen it.

They watched curiously as she sat in the chair across from him. A small table separated them. He didn't say anything. He knew everyone in that bar watched him with as much scrutiny as they watched her. He wouldn't speak first no matter how much he wanted to start figuring out how he'd get back home. Let her set the parameters of their engagement.

"I'm Shira," she said for the second time that night. "This is my pack. Since you're my guest, don't you think you owe me a name?"

Noah considered giving her the number tattooed on his arm. But baiting her would be stupid right now if he still wanted her help. He needed transportation and a plan. If her pack had been holed up here a while—and it looked as if they had—they'd know where he could get the things he needed for the trip.

He watched her discomfort grow as he stared at her. Finally he said, "Noah."

She still wore the black leather pants her pack had tossed her. But she'd changed into a more revealing top and had added boots and some gold jewelry to the mix. And make-up. Her smokey eyes and bright red lips were an orchestrated seduction, meant to draw him in. She formed her words slowly, and leaned in toward him.

"So, how did you meet the girl?"

Noah stared at Shira, his expression closed. He wasn't going to play this game. Sydney wasn't her business, and he wouldn't give the alpha even the smallest tidbit of information that she could use in whatever her plan was. But he thought he knew. Though he'd been blocked off from the world, there were some things you just knew without knowing how you knew them.

When she saw she wasn't getting anywhere via that route, she unbuttoned another button on her top. "Wow, it's hot in here. The desert. You never get used to this heat."

If that was the case, she shouldn't be wearing leather pants and boots. Werewolves ran hotter, anyway.

She scooted her chair closer and ran a long red fingernail down the side of Noah's throat.

He growled. "I told you, Sydney is mine."

"You haven't marked her," Shira said.

"Not yet."

"And even so, it doesn't mean you can only have one. You can have whatever you want. Why don't we move this conversation somewhere more private?"

Someone casually observing might guess that her

desire for privacy was rooted in seduction, but Noah sensed it was because she feared he'd shoot her down in front of her pack. After all, he'd already given her a warning growl.

"I'm fine right here," he said.

She leaned in even closer, her breasts brushing his arm as she whispered, "She's too weak for you. You and I could run this pack."

"Why? Because you're afraid I'll try to take it from you otherwise? Don't worry, I have no designs on your pack."

"A bit presumptuous don't you think? I run a big pack with several decent fighters. You think they'd submit to my leadership if I weren't strong enough to lead? This isn't the human world. I couldn't have slept my way to the top even if I'd wanted to. You saw me reclaim my human form out there when no one else could."

Noah turned fully toward her, pinning her to her seat with a glare. "I know we both sized each other up out there under the moon. I was born in my fur. Tonight is my twenty-eighth birth moon. And it's a blood moon. I escaped a heavily guarded facility, leaving dozens of bodies in my wake. You might be strong enough to lead, but we both know you're just trying to seduce me because you think I'm going to take your pack from you. Between us, you know I would win in a challenge fight. And I think you're smart enough to know I wouldn't pull my punches. After all, it would be disrespect to hold back just because you're a woman when you've proven you can hold a pack on your own."

Her manipulative pout morphed into a snarl. "I

shouldn't have extended hospitality to you. I should have just let you and your girl die out in the desert. Between the vampires and the human magic users coming from the city, they would have ripped you apart."

Noah shrugged. "Just turn off the seduction routine. I'm not interested in you or your pack. I just need a mode of transportation, a map, and some supplies." He still wasn't clear on what supplies he might need, but if he just said *supplies*, maybe they would magically come together in a bag for him. Let her lackeys sort out what kind of supplies he needed. They knew the area. There was no reason to show his ignorance. It would be another sign of weakness.

She sighed. "Fine. Truth be told, I want you out of my space."

He very much doubted that. He'd smelled her when he'd first shifted in the lobby. She wanted to jump on him. If she took a mate, most likely she'd fall back to second in command, and none of the wolves in this pack seemed like someone she'd want to take a ruling back-seat to. But someone new, someone with power? Maybe. Though, despite her desire for Noah, there was also some truth to her words. She wanted to be the alpha, not second string of an alpha pair. And if she'd back the hell off, he would happily get out of her space and let her carry on as the queen or however she saw herself.

"Rafe," Shira said over the music in the bar. "My room. Now."

Rafe perked up at that and practically raced out of the bar. They'd all watched Noah turn her down, so now she had to prove she could still make any one of those wolves jump into her bed on cue. And most likely she could. She certainly had her charms.

Noah stayed where he was, irritated that they were no closer to getting the things he needed to get Sydney out of here. He'd wanted to leave the following evening as soon as she rose. They were still far too close to the facility they'd been held captive in for his comfort. But the possibility of getting out at sunset was beginning to seem less realistic.

His nostrils flared when he smelled Sydney in the lobby. He'd told her to stay in their room. He stalked out of the bar, livid that she hadn't listened to him when he was trying to keep her safe. He could have thrown her down and marked her the second he had her. It would have protected her, but he was trying not to be a monster about it. What could she be thinking in this place with all these strange wolves? This wasn't his dad's well-behaved pack.

When he reached the lobby, he stopped dead in his tracks. The heavy metal screaming through the speakers that once were used for train announcements, made it hard for him to concentrate. All he could do was growl.

Two of the male wolves had dragged Sydney down here. He wasn't sure if she'd left her room on her own, but the smell of fear on her made him somehow doubt it.

"What is the meaning of this?" Shira said, but her act wasn't fooling Noah. He could tell by the way her body went rigid that she'd orchestrated it. She'd thought things would go a different direction and had forgotten to call off her dogs.

"But Shira, you said…"

"Release her this instant," the alpha said.

Noah tensed, every instinct telling him to rip them all apart. But even if he thought there was some small chance he could do that, or at least could take out enough of them to intimidate the rest, it was too risky. Maybe this could be diffused another way. Maybe the cheery robotic voice had given him a sense of diplomacy over the years, no matter how artificial. If he'd used it once before to survive, he could use it now.

Sydney's eyes glowed red and her fangs descended. She growled low in her throat. It was a menacing sound Noah never thought he would hear from her. She spun on one of her captors, hauled back, and landed a hard punch to his jaw. He reeled back.

Sydney stared at her fist, stunned. "I-I don't know where that came from."

The wolf she'd punched advanced on her and growled.

That was Noah's cue. He shifted and pounced on top of the guy. The other wolf shifted as he got thrown to the ground and the two of them rolled around on the floor, snapping and snarling, blood flying out from the fight until the other wolf let out a horrible wail and became very still.

Noah was about to shift back to normal when Shira shifted and jumped on him. It wasn't the fight he'd asked for or the fight he wanted, but it was the one he had. She was tougher than the male he'd just killed, and he knew without doubt as they fought, that she'd been strong enough to lead this pack. But she wasn't strong enough to beat Noah.

His fangs dug into her as she shifted back, and he let go. She scrambled away, clutching at her throat, but it was obvious from the look in her eyes that she knew it was too late for her.

Noah shifted back and wiped the blood off his mouth. "You should have let us be on our way without the theatrics. It didn't have to go this way. I didn't want it to."

The light left her eyes, and she stared sightlessly up from the floor.

The metal that had raged through the speakers, stopped, and the room fell quiet. The wolves that had been in the lounge, filed into the lobby. Noah moved in front of Sydney.

One by one, they dropped to one knee and bared their throats.

"We're going back to our room," Noah said, trying to ignore that about forty wolves had just pledged their fealty to him. No matter what his instincts said, he couldn't lead a pack. He barely remembered how pack dynamics worked. He had some deep issues from being in that place. He'd only abuse those in his care. If he had a pack, he wanted to be like his dad. He didn't want it like this. And he had to get back home so his family knew he was alive.

His parents would have had a memorial in honor of what would have been his coming-of-age birth moon. Tonight. They were mourning tonight, and he had a pack wanting him to lead them. It was too messed up.

One of the wolves rose and moved hesitantly toward him. "Um... sir, we have a much nicer room for the alpha to stay in. That room you've been in isn't good enough for..."

Noah held back a growl as the wolf moved closer to Sydney than he was comfortable with after what almost just happened. What *had* almost just happened? He still wasn't sure what Shira's plan had been, but whatever it was had proven incredibly foolish. Perhaps she'd planned to get rid of Sydney and then execute the wolves who'd taken her, pretending they'd acted alone and not on her orders.

The other wolf took a couple of steps back.

"We aren't staying. We're leaving as soon as the sun is down and we can arrange transport."

"We'll go with you," another wolf said. They were getting braver.

"Why? I don't want a pack." That was a lie. "I was only protecting my mate." *The mate I haven't marked yet.* He wasn't even a fit mate. If he was, he would have done what was necessary to protect her first, before anything else, rather than treating her like they were a couple of humans on a date trying to see if maybe the other might be The One.

He'd known Sydney was the one. She knew it, too. Giving her a few days to make it seem as if fate hadn't already decided for them only put her at risk—particularly when she couldn't hold her own with anyone stronger than another frail human female. Although... she'd just thrown a pretty harsh right hook, most likely courtesy of his blood. And that was just from feeding once.

"S-sir, we need a leader. We're willing to go with you,

wherever you want. Anyone else here leading will be weaker than Shira. And while she was strong, our pack isn't as secure as it could be. It will be less so if we follow someone else. It'll be safer for you and your mate to travel with a pack."

What was the likelihood they'd willingly help him and Sydney get out of here if he rejected them? Probably not high. After all, if he flat out said no, whether they wanted to follow him or not, they could collectively turn on him and take the trash out.

He sighed. "Honestly, who here wants to come with us and establish a pack farther north near my family? Show of hands?" Maybe if he framed it that way, more would hesitate, and they'd get off this kick. Shira wasn't even cold yet.

One by one hands raised until all were in the air, but the last few were more fear than truly wanting to go.

"Fine. Get what we need together and we'll go at sunset. What do you have for transportation?"

"Motorcycles," one of them said.

Noah quickly covered his reaction. He couldn't even drive a car. Where would he have learned? He'd thought if they had cars, one of them could act as his and Sydney's driver and no one had to know just how cut off from the whole world he'd been. They were going to figure out he was a fraud before they got out of the gate. And that would put Sydney at risk.

"O-only... sir... if we could just wait until after the moon begins to wane. We can't all travel in human form under the full moon. M-most of us can't. We need to wait until we have better control. And we'll better be able to prepare for the journey."

And they'd be much less likely to rip Noah and Sydney apart when they realized their new savior wasn't so fit for leadership after all. They'd been far better off with Shira.

Noah looked around at the assembled, anxious wolves. "We'll leave on the first night of the waning moon at sunset. Anyone who doesn't want to be a part of my pack can stay behind. There will be no retaliation for anyone who chooses to stay." He had two nights to figure out how to ride a motorcycle and even less time to mark Sydney. Two nights was plenty of time for them to all defect, anyway.

7

Sydney tensed as Noah guided her back to their room. Surely he knew she hadn't just walked out of there under her own steam. And if there was any doubt, the shattered door was proof enough there had been a struggle.

One of the other wolves lurked out in the hallway. "Umm, sir? About that other room..."

Noah growled in response, but took Sydney and followed the wolf up a couple of flights of stairs to a large suite. The wolf quickly ducked out and Noah deadbolted the door and put a chair under it.

Sydney searched the suite, looking for a place she'd feel safe for the day. The other room had been better from her perspective with no way any sunlight could get in through solid wall and brick.

She settled on the bathroom. She could take the comforter and pillows off one of the beds and put it in the giant tub. The bathroom was enormous with no windows.

Noah stood back and watched as she made what could only be described as a nest for herself in the bathtub. He didn't say anything. Was he angry?

"Noah, I-I'm sorry about all that out there."

He raised an eyebrow. "What do you have to be sorry for?"

"Well, I mean… if I hadn't hit that guy… I escalated things, but I just… I got so angry. I've never been that angry before, I'm not sure why…"

"It was my blood. You've never drank from a werewolf before, have you?"

She shook her head. "Therians don't usually line up to volunteer as blood dolls for us, and it wasn't as if I could do anything to change that."

Although… when she'd hit the guy, her hand hadn't even hurt. And she'd definitely done damage. There was no way she should have been able to do that. She looked up to find Noah still watching her closely.

"I don't think you're going to stay very weak for long," Noah said. "Earlier, you healed fast, even old scars. Then you hit that wolf. And that's just from feeding one time. Once I've marked you, and you've had even more… over time I think you'll be strong like a normal vampire."

A normal vampire.

Sydney could barely dare to dream that she had the smallest hope of being normal. She'd lived so long having to be under someone's protective wing that the idea of ever being able to hold her own with anyone seemed as unlikely as unicorns.

"Sydney..."

"Yeah?" The way he looked at her, all wild intensity and purpose, made her glad she wasn't going to be an entirely helpless damsel for long. It wasn't that she feared him. He was Noah. But still.

"I need to mark you."

"You said..."

She'd thought as long as she didn't escalate things to sex between them, a feat in and of itself for her when it came to feeding, that there would be time to get used to the idea. Not that she didn't want to be with him. It was just that... when she'd run away from home, she hadn't realized she was running straight into the arms of her future werewolf mate. Even if it sounded like a good idea, a lot had happened in a short time, and she still worried he might be wrong. Surely being locked up like that for so long had skewed his sense of... well, everything. They hadn't talked about it, but she could see how he reacted around others. Slight shifts in body language that nobody else paid attention to because they had other worries to deal with than decoding the body language of the stranger among them.

But Sydney remembered Noah from when they were kids. He hadn't been quiet like this. He hadn't been closed off, wanting to be alone all the time. He'd been the center of attention, charismatic, gregarious. That place had changed him. She still wanted him, but what if some day he realized that he didn't want her? That she'd only been a bit of comfort for when nothing else around him had smelled like home.

If he later discovered someone else was his true

mate... she'd claw the bitch's eyes out. Whoa. Yeah, were-wolf blood. Damn. How did Noah control this? It was as if she now had her own wolf that had grafted onto her. A little angry furry Sydney to contend with. All the impotent rage that had built within her over years of powerlessness. The anger she'd had to tamp down because she wasn't strong enough to back it up with an arsenal of bad ass. Someone else always had to fight her battles.

Now that she thought about it... she wasn't sorry at all for hitting that guy. He'd had it coming. She only regretted that it had set up a situation it didn't seem Noah wanted. Without meaning to, she'd handed him a huge level of responsibility, and maybe he just wanted to go back home and live with his pack and try to find some way to recover from twenty years in that terrible glass cube.

She wouldn't have made it twenty days without losing her mind. Noah was strong in more ways than he realized.

"Sydney?"

"Yeah?" She'd kind of just spaced out there and wondered how long she'd been having an internal monologue, grateful wolves couldn't read minds like vampires could. Or most vampires, anyway.

"Look, I know what I said, but if I had marked you when we first got here you might have been safer. And with the pack now, if I don't mark you, you definitely won't be safe from the women. They'll all fight to be alpha bitch."

Sydney was doubtful. Wolves tended to respect the marks of other wolves, but it wasn't as if they had to, particularly when a stranger was among a pack that wasn't his. Under ordinary circumstances it was respected, but if the pack's alpha had ordered an execution, it wouldn't have kept her safe. Noah had to know that.

Even among vampires, while a vampire physically couldn't feed on a claimed mate because of the mystical protection it placed upon the other, it didn't mean a vampire wouldn't just separate the human's head from his or her body if they felt like it.

Sydney's eyes went to Noah's throat. She licked her lips at the pounding, surging warm blood that hummed just beneath the surface of his skin. In the years that followed, she would likely rewind to this day and try to pick apart her motivations to figure out why exactly she'd done what she did next, but the only answer that would likely ever come to her was... instinct.

Without thinking, she launched herself at him and sank her fangs into his throat. She took a couple of pulls of his blood, then pricked her own tongue with her fang and quickly, before his wound could close, mixed their blood.

She pulled back and felt the fierce red glow in her eyes, and she said: "Mine."

The second the word was out of her mouth, Noah's eyes glowed yellow and he growled at her. Growled. At her. She would have punched *him* in the jaw, except she wasn't fast enough. He tackled her, and before she could think, his fangs were in her throat.

He growled again, and she felt the control he was trying to gain. That growl was angry. It wasn't excited or even possessive. It was rage, and she was possibly about two seconds from getting her throat ripped out.

"Noah," she said quietly.

His tongue trailed over her neck, then he pulled back, his eyes glowing golden. "Mine," he snarled, still half-angry.

Well. Okay then. At least he'd gotten control of himself and hadn't ripped her throat out. But the confrontation wasn't over. Not by a long shot.

He struggled to his feet and glared at her for a second, then he went outside on the balcony. Sydney glanced at the clock. It was about an hour until the sun came up, but she wasn't even tired yet. Normally she'd already be asleep, the soon-approaching sun already draining her well before it could peak over the horizon and start its ascent into the sky. A few vampires out there were so strong that they could, from a sheltered and shaded place, watch the first red hints of dawn climb into the sky before falling dead for the day. Sydney had always believed she'd never be that strong, that the only sunrise she'd ever see was a manufactured or pre-recorded one playing on a screen. Now she had her doubts.

This had been the longest night of her life, and she was very aware of how close it had been to being her last. Twice. It hurt that the biggest threat to her that second time had been the man who'd claimed she was his *true mate*. What did he know about true mates after being locked up like that? He hadn't even been raised by wolves properly.

She didn't follow him outside. She didn't even want

to see him right now. For better or worse they were tied together. Instead, she went to the bathroom. She wasn't sure how long she'd manage to stay awake, but the clock was ticking down and if she had any hope of making it until sunset, she had to be in the safety of the bathroom when she fell dead for the day.

Sydney wasn't even sure she'd be safe like that, so vulnerable with Noah right there. She resented that he was her only protection, and he was behaving like some rabid animal she couldn't trust. She ran her fingers over the mark he'd left on her throat as she looked at it in the mirror. She could see the vampiric demon rippling under the surface in her reflection. The image had never been this strong before. It had been the tiniest ghost of a thing before when she'd looked in a mirror, nothing like her dad's reflection which was strong and looked to be more demon than human half the time.

She could already see the vampire side of her growing stronger. If she'd somehow fed from Noah before they'd escaped the city, she had a feeling the barrier would have recognized her as a preternatural and wouldn't have let her pass.

The place where Noah had bitten her glowed in the mirror. He'd marked her as his mate. There was no doubt about that. So she should be safe when she went to sleep. Right? The rage rose up again, and she smashed the mirror. She watched as her bleeding hand healed before her eyes. Yes, she was definitely different now.

The bathroom door flew open as Noah raced inside. "What happened? Are you okay?"

"You almost ripped my throat out, and now you're

asking if I'm okay? I'm fine. Please leave me alone." She climbed into the tub and propped up all her pillows. "And shut that door when you leave. We can't let any sunlight in."

Noah shut the bathroom door and sat on the closed toilet lid. "I'm not going anywhere. I'm staying right here until you rise for the night."

"Don't be ridiculous. When was the last time you ate something? You need to hunt."

Something flickered over his face, and then she realized... he hadn't hunted anything since he was a pup. And back then he'd just been learning. Literally everything had to be so hard for him right now. What else had he not experienced that most others his age would have?

"I'll be fine. I'm sure I can get one of my new underlings to bring me something." He crossed his arms stubbornly over his chest.

Several minutes passed in silence, and then he said, "Sydney, why would you do that? A pack just surrendered to me, and you *claimed* me! In the first place, you're a vampire. No wolf pack is going to accept a vampire as the alpha. And in the second place, you might be stronger now than you started out, but you aren't strong enough to hold a pack, and if it looks like you control me, they won't accept me, either. Not that I care, but it's better that they want to follow us than kill us. Don't you think?"

This may have been more words than he'd ever strung together at one time since they'd been reunited.

"And you marked me back," Sydney said. "So it's okay. Your mark took. And I know my claim did."

He put his head in his hands, then looked up. "Again, Sydney, why? Why would you claim me? Do you know how close I came to ripping your throat out before I marked you? The wolf saw that as a challenge. Why would you do that? You've been around wolves enough to know better. Or maybe it's been so long you've forgotten."

Sydney wasn't sure why she'd done it. It had been instinct. It wasn't like she'd had a pro/con list or some grand plan, but reasons that made sense began to crystallize in her mind now that everything had settled. She wasn't entirely sure that any of these reasons were *why* she'd done it, since she hadn't planned it, but she could throw it out there and see if any of it made sense to Noah —if any of it could smooth this out.

"How much do you remember about your parents?" she asked.

"Huh?"

She took a deep breath and plunged in. "I know your mom's a demon, but she was human in the beginning. Do you remember when your dad talked about how when he marked your mom it didn't extend her life past a human life span because wolf marks don't work that way?"

"Yeah, so?"

"So, if she hadn't ended up a demon, their lifespans wouldn't have matched up, and at some point they would have lost each other forever. I didn't know at first, but while I was in that place, they ran some tests and found out I'd stopped aging. So I won't get old, but in a few hundred years, you would. Maybe that sounds like forever to us now, but if you were right and you were going to mark me and tie us together, how would I feel when you died and left me? Shouldn't we have the potential to have lifespans that match? You won't age now. At all. If this was going to happen, I had to make sure that wouldn't come back and bite us later like it did for your dad."

Noah sighed. "But my mom was already dad's mate when she later became a demon, and then because of their link he became immortal, too. And I heard that when Hadrian claimed Angeline, he got true immortality because guardians don't die. So it might have happened anyway, even if I'd just marked you because of you being already immortal."

"Maybe. But what if it didn't? Or what if I couldn't claim you after you marked me? If I'm your true mate, you should be happy about it, that we don't have to worry about that later."

"We should have talked about it first," Noah said.

"Oh like you were going to just *talk* about marking me? I saw that look in your eyes. You weren't gearing up for a reasoned conversation. You were intent on marking me right then. I had to do it then or never."

Noah went to the sink. He gripped the edge of the counter and stared into the shattered mirror. Their eyes met in a fragment of the reflection.

"Sydney, I don't think I can give you what you need. I'm not good for you. I'm not good for this pack. I can't do all this."

She growled from the pile of blankets in the tub. "Well now is a fucking great time for that after—"

Then everything went black.

Sydney opened her eyes, snuggled in the blankets in the tub, a large, warm furry body curled protectively around her. She glanced over to see animal bones near the sink, and blood on the tile floor. One of the other wolves must have brought him something to eat during the day.

She hadn't even been in the tub when she was yelling at him. She imagined Noah catching her as she went down and wrapping her in the blankets. She wondered if he'd shifted to feed or because he was stronger in his wolf form and could better protect her. Either way, she knew he hadn't left her side all day.

It was hard to stay angry at him under the circumstances. He couldn't give her what she needed? Sydney thought maybe he could do a lot more than he thought he could. He'd done what needed to be done to get them out of there and find them shelter. He'd killed his own kind to protect her. When she'd smashed the mirror, he'd put aside anger and confusion to rush in there. And now, here he was guarding her.

Sydney ran her fingers through his fur. It reminded her of when they were kids, before he'd shifted for the first time. She'd woken up like this so often when they were young, with the wolf wrapped around her, guarding her. It was understandable why maybe she and Noah wouldn't have understood there was something deeper in their connection, but had their parents not even seen it?

Or maybe they had seen it and had disapproved. Maybe that was why they'd been separated. And maybe there was still another reason she'd claimed him. When they got back they were going to have to deal with their families. Amidst happy reunions there could be disapproval from either or both sets of parents. Werewolves and vampires weren't known to be very best friends, after all. There was the occasional odd alliance, but it wasn't a normal way for them to interact.

If her father didn't approve of this match, Sydney knew he'd try to separate them again. He wouldn't care if Noah had marked her. But a claim was something different. He wouldn't try to separate them with a claim in place no matter how much he might hate it. Even so, it would be better to keep that side of her reasons to herself. Noah wouldn't appreciate hearing how to Anthony, her claim trumped his mark, not when they'd had their first fight over that same subject. With wolves, she was sure that the mark on her throat was enough. It was possible they wouldn't realize there was also a vampire claim in play.

After all, Noah's mark was pretty screamingly obvious—and not a gentle one. It was the one mark on her that wouldn't ever heal. Her father would be livid when he saw it.

Sydney nudged the wolf. He yawned and stretched and buried his nose inside the blankets. She was hungry and she wasn't about to sink fangs into fur. Gross.

"Noah!"

He made a snorting sound and snuggled some more.

"Hey! Wake up!" Seriously? If she were under attack, she wondered if he'd sleep right through it.

He stretched again and shifted into his human form.

"Hey," he said. He was over it, too. Maybe she should schedule all their fights for right before she fell dead for the day. It wasn't the most healthy communication strategy, but it worked.

He kissed her over his mark and growled against her throat. "You hungry?"

For everything. Naked hot werewolf mate draped over her at the moment. There hadn't exactly been time or mood to be amorous when they'd marked each other. There wasn't time for fighting and make-up sex. There hadn't even been time to finish fighting.

His erection pressed against her through the blankets.

"Let's relocate," she said. It was a huge tub, but with all the blankets and pillows, it was too cramped for anything but sleep.

Sydney watched as he stood and stretched. Oh, she could get used to this view every night. He reached down and helped her stand. She opened the door to go into the main room but leaped back out of the way and slammed it.

Noah moved in front of the door to stay between her and whatever was on the other side. She knew he hadn't smelled anyone. There wasn't anyone to smell.

"What is it?"

"The sun," Sydney said. "It's not down yet." She didn't even think vampires could wake up before the sun went down. Of course, she didn't know any vampires mated to werewolves, either.

"Stay here, I'll be right back." Noah stepped out of the room for a few minutes and then came back in. "The sun is setting now. It should be safe in about twenty minutes or so."

"Still, I shouldn't be able to even wake up before it goes down. Normally I slept a few hours past sunset." She'd always been the last vampire to rise.

Noah got the blankets and pillows out of the tub and started moving them into the other room. "I'll let you know when it's safe."

Sydney peeled off her clothes and got in the shower. A few minutes later, she sensed Noah. She felt his eyes on her through the glass, but he didn't make a move to join her.

"Sun's down," he said. "You can come out any time. There's a bathrobe on the tub, and Shira's got a ton of clothes in the closet that would probably fit you."

Sydney wrinkled her nose at the idea of wearing the clothes of a dead woman, but it would be a lot better than the awful white clothes she'd had to wear since living in that glass cube. She'd looked like a cult member.

The door clicked closed. Really? He'd said she was his true mate. She was naked in a hot shower with water dripping off her. He wasn't getting in with her?

Then she realized... *Noah's never... He's a virgin.* He'd been taken as a kid, and the robot voice had seriously discouraged all fraternizing. When would he have had an opportunity? Of course he wouldn't just jump her in the shower.

She shut off the water and grabbed a towel to dry off. She glanced briefly at the bathrobe, but left it draped where it was. The wolf was clearly going to need some encouragement.

When she stepped out, she gasped. Flowers and candles filled the room. Noah was still lighting a few of them.

"After the way I spoke to you last night, the way I spoke to you at that place, I wanted tonight to be special. You haven't had a chance to see my very best side," he said.

The man had no idea how sweet he was. After everything he must have been through, being isolated from his family and other close social contact that wolves needed to be halfway normal—for years—and he was apologizing for all the stress he was under.

Sydney dropped the towel and stalked him across the room. "It's just me. I used to tug on your fur when I was a baby. You don't have to impress me."

A long breath spiraled out of him, as if he'd been holding it since they were children. He wrapped his arms around her and held her for a long time. He smelled clean and fresh from the shower. She wondered if he'd gone next door for that.

He wore only a pair of sweatpants—no shirt or shoes. She wanted to snuggle into him forever.

"You should feed."

The pulse danced in his throat, calling to her. She very much doubted that she ever could have taken enough of Noah's blood to endanger him, particularly when he was strong enough to throw her off him, but now with the claim, there was no way she could take too much.

"Are you still mad at me?"

He kissed the top of her head. "I was never mad *at* you. I was worried for you. I was afraid if the wolves knew, they might turn on us. I don't know how that would go. I need to keep you safe."

Sydney's nose wrinkled as she looked into his eyes. "Really? Because I don't remember it exactly that way."

He sighed. "Part of it was just irrational macho wolf stuff. Okay? Is that what you want to hear? But that's not *me*. That's not how *I* feel. It was just an instinct. Are you still mad at me?"

In answer, she gripped the back of his neck and pulled his mouth to hers.

"Y-you need to feed," he murmured.

"Oh, I can do both. Just let me take care of you." Sydney shoved him back on the bed. She knew he was nervous, that he had to worry he wasn't wolf enough for her because he hadn't had a million conquests before. And she had experience.

When she shoved him back, he went because something had changed in her when they'd bonded and she'd fed from him. There was no doubt now that she'd be a normal vampire. She'd shoved him, and it had actually moved him. Unlike the weak push that wouldn't have budged him two nights ago.

He seemed impressed, and she flushed. But then she was more interested in other things. "You had to have done more than just run in the exercise yard all those years."

"I might have lifted a few weights on occasion," he said.

She laughed. "Such modesty."

"I'm a wolf. There isn't a modest bone in my body."

Like most of his kind, they didn't shy away from or get weird about nudity. Even captivity hadn't changed that trait. He'd put on the sweatpants for her comfort, not his. She pulled them off and drank in the sight of him.

That is yours. Forever, a dark voice in her mind whispered.

She straddled him and licked those perfectly chiseled abs and the lovely lines that framed his hips. His cock jumped when her tongue stroked it. He gripped the mattress so hard, his claws were starting to come out, and so was the mattress stuffing.

"You poor deprived thing," she teased.

He chuckled. "What have I gotten myself into?"

Sydney slid up his body and positioned herself over him. She let out a sharp whimper when she took him inside her. He was so warm. Much warmer than a human. Their eyes met.

"You okay?" he asked.

She felt the blush rise up her throat and into her face. "Yes. You're just warmer than I'm used to..." *Way to kill the mood, Sydney.* "I'm sorry, I shouldn't have said that."

Noah's hand rested on the side of her cheek. "Hey. I don't care. You're mine now. Nothing before that matters. I know sex and feeding often go together with vampires. You didn't know I was your mate. You didn't even know I was alive. I would never expect you to be miserable or alone. Ever. Okay?"

She nodded and began to move. She smiled when his

breathing became more erratic, then she let her fangs come out and bit him. She hadn't realized how hungry she'd been. This time it wasn't overwhelming. He tasted like peace and love and comfort and safety, and she couldn't believe she'd been drinking anything less for all these years.

Lust and tenderness, protectiveness and love made the blood sweeter than anything she'd ever had before. His hands dug into her hips, and a moment later he'd flipped the two of them.

The combination of his blood and the way his body rubbed against hers, sent her spiraling into the best orgasm of her life. It caused her fangs to clamp down harder, urged her to drink more deeply as she bucked and writhed underneath him.

He let out a roar when he came.

"Wow," he said, as he collapsed on top of her.

She laughed and licked the last bits of blood that strayed down his throat.

They laid sprawled together for several minutes, and then Sydney started to cry. "I thought for years that I was never going to see you again."

Noah held her hands in his. "Mates always find each other. Always. Destiny pulled you to me."

Sydney wanted to say that was nonsense, but she wasn't so sure right now. If Jacob hadn't betrayed her and taken her to the city, would Noah have been motivated enough to fight so hard to get out?

"We should go downstairs," he said. "I need to get a sense of how loyal they're still feeling after they've had time to sleep on it."

Noah pulled the sweatpants back on and blew out the candles around the room. Sydney forced herself to get out of the fluffy bed and went to Shira's closet to find something to wear.

"Holy crap. This chick had a ton of knives." Sydney gawked at the rows and rows of sharp, pointy weapons designed to do maximum damage and the array of holsters to conceal them. "Why would she have all this when she had claws?"

Noah poked his head in. "It's not always convenient to shift to wolf form for fighting. With her size, she prob-ably took all the advantages she could find." He left Sydney alone in the closet to continue her search.

He was right, the alpha had been just about her size. It wasn't a perfect match, but it was close enough that nothing but the most form-fitting clothing would reveal an ill-fit.

She chose a red tank top and jeans from the closet, making sure the top displayed Noah's mark. They'd smell it on her, of course, but she wanted them to see it. If they saw how hard he'd marked her, it could only make him look better. Then maybe they wouldn't notice her claim simmering just below the surface.

The mark she'd left on him wouldn't heal, either. But hers was more discreet.

"Maybe you want to cover that," she said.

He stared at his reflection in the mirror, then shrugged. "Or maybe I don't. They'll find out eventually. It'll look weak to slink around in the shadows covering it. I'm not doing a thing, and if anyone has anything to say, they can get their ass beat."

"I'm not sure I want to beat any asses right now," Sydney said.

"Smart ass."

She rifled through the drawers in the bathroom until she found a brush and some hair sticks. She ran the brush through her long blonde hair and then put it up in a bun with the sticks. She found some brown boots in the closet and added some jewelry.

"Are you going to the mall?" Noah asked.

"I can't even believe you know what a mall is. No. I just thought, if we're really doing this thing with the pack, I can't look hesitant about wearing or using anything that belonged to the former alpha. We have to lay claim to everything. Isn't that how wolves think?"

"Yeah. That's how they think. You'll fit right in."

"Or I'll beat asses." They both knew these weren't idle words. Sydney wasn't sure if he realized it, but drinking a full normal amount from him had made her even stronger. She was confident she could hold her own with most of the wolves lower in the hierarchy. And she could bluff with the others.

When they reached the lobby, Sydney was underwhelmed. No one was down there. There was only one wolf in the bar. Had they deserted? Maybe they'd gone hunting. It *was* the full moon, still. But from what she knew, the alpha led the hunt on the full moon. Packs didn't just wander off on their own without permission.

The guy behind the bar stepped out, nervously. "T-they were supposed to be back before sunset."

"Where. Are. They?" Noah said, sounding very much like the asshole who'd called her by a number instead of a name in the exercise yard, back when she'd thought he might bust through the glass and kill her. "Rafe?" he growled.

Rafe was visibly shaking.

"Did they go on the hunt?"

The other wolf shook his head. When he spoke again, his voice came out barely above a whisper. It was hard to discern his words over the metal pounding through the lobby. "T-they went to bury her."

NOAH GROWLED and Rafe jumped back as if he'd caught on fire. He thought the other wolf might piss his pants. Good. It wasn't that Noah cared about them burying Shira. She'd been their alpha, maybe even for a long time. Giving her a proper burial ceremony was the right thing to do and would facilitate the transition that much easier with no bad blood. But they should have gotten permission first.

The fact that they'd slunk off to do it in the day behind his back was not a good thing. And he had no idea how he'd handle it. If he went on a killing rampage, they'd all fear him. If he acted like it was no big deal, he'd never hold the pack.

"S-sir?"

"WHAT?"

Rafe cringed again, and something in Noah just wanted to kill the weak fucker, but then, he'd been the only one who'd stayed behind. Why punish that?

"I tried to tell them to wait and ask, but they were

afraid you'd say no. Shira meant a lot to the pack. She kept us together and out of trouble for a long time."

"If they liked her so much, why did they all so quickly jump to follow me?"

"No one else in this group is much of a leader. And we need a strong leader to survive out here."

If only they knew how long he'd been kept in that cell. They wouldn't be turning to him to save them all. There was only so far brute strength could take him. And the half-faded, barely there memories of how his dad ran things weren't going to help him now, anyway. His dad had run an established pack for decades. This wasn't the same situation at all. He had no idea how to gain their trust *and* respect.

One or the other would have been easier, but to put the fear of God in them while also gaining their trust and loyalty wasn't the most realistic task he'd ever been assigned.

Sydney squeezed his hand. And that was yet *another* issue. If he came off weak, someone might try to hurt her, even with his mark.

Wolves began running in through the revolving doors and shifting back to their human forms. Noah let go of Sydney's hand and crossed his arms over his chest. He let out a low growl.

"Who is responsible for this?"

The pack members looked at the ground.

"Should I just start killing until one of you talks?"

Sydney let out a shocked gasp. Noah rounded on her and glared. He wished he could make her understand, but she had to stand with him now. Thankfully she closed her mouth and masked whatever emotions she was working through. He couldn't reassure her. Every eye was on him, determining if he was fit to lead, determining if they could trust him. He wondered if this rebellion wasn't a test, rather than an actual rebellion. After all, what were their other options right now?

If he and Sydney just left them, what would they do? There was no one else to lead. The pack would fall apart and they'd fall prey to the vampires lurking in the area. Possibly some of them would be taken by the magic users into the city. If they scattered and tried to get farther from the city, they'd just run into unfamiliar territory. They wouldn't survive without each other and an alpha. Of course it was a test.

"Rafe, shut that shit off." Noah pointed up at the speakers still pounding out the metal.

The wolf that had stayed behind scrambled to obey the order.

"WHO is responsible?" His voice echoed off the walls.

He didn't have to bluff. If these wolves were going to pose a threat or problem for him or Sydney, he had no qualms about taking them out. And judging from the fear in the room, they wouldn't be able to organize well enough to overtake him. They'd hesitate. And that would be enough. From the looks on their faces, they all knew he wasn't just putting on a show.

One of the wolves stepped out of the pack.

"It was me. Shira was my sister."

Noah shouldn't have been surprised that it was a female wolf. Between his mother and Shira, it wasn't as if the idea was all that shocking. But from what he'd gleaned, statistically male wolves tended to be stronger, and they also tended to cause more trouble.

"Livia!" one of the other wolves snapped.

"He'd kill me when he found out, anyway. Isn't it better to keep the rest of you safe?"

Traditionally when a new alpha came in, they didn't just take out the former alpha, but any close blood relations that might cause problems in the new structure. Given what she'd already done, it wasn't crazy for her to think she was about to die. But if he killed her, he'd look like a monster. He might have their fear, but he'd never gain their trust.

"Come here."

She stepped away from the group and approached him. Noah allowed himself to shift just enough for his claws to come out. The room went absolutely silent. Even Sydney didn't make a sound. Livia squeezed her eyes shut and cringed. Instead of slitting her throat like another alpha would have, his claws sliced through her shoulder, leaving a trail of blood and torn flesh behind.

Noah watched as the blood slowed, but she didn't heal. His suspicions about this pack were right. Acting collectively as a pack, they were fine, but none of them alone or even in small groups could challenge him. Livia wouldn't heal properly until she'd had something to eat. Even then, it might take a day or two.

"You will never defy me like that again. Is that understood?"

"Y-yes, sir."

"I would have let you bury her if you'd asked."

Noah turned back to the group and gestured to his mate. "If any of you don't know, I'm Noah. Sydney and I are your new alphas. You are not lone wolves. You don't take a piss without one of us knowing about it from now on. Are we clear?"

All throughout the large lobby, werewolves dropped to one knee and bared their throats. Except a small cluster at the back. He wasn't surprised he didn't have one hundred percent support. Especially after marking a vampire. Noah wasn't sure if the group had noticed the mark Sydney had left on him, but it was none of their business.

"No," one of the wolves in the back said, still standing, his arms crossed over his chest. "I'm not answering to a *vampire*. I've had to do a lot of things in my life for survival, but that's not going to be one of them."

Before Noah could say anything else, Sydney had blurred across the floor and shoved the wolf back hard. He landed with a loud crack as his tailbone hit the ground.

"Yes. You will," she said, growling for emphasis.

Noah couldn't be prouder. She understood things. But then, she'd been raised by the vampire king who, from the stories that had circulated in the exercise yard over the years, still made quite an impression on people. She was her father's daughter, and she knew the game they had to play now.

The small cluster of hold outs dropped to one knee and bared their throats. Slowly the male who had spoken up joined them.

"Any further questions?" Noah asked as Sydney

calmly made her way back to his side. He nodded his approval at her.

When no one made a sound he asked, "Did you hunt without me?"

Heads shook quickly.

"Good. Let's go. Livia, stay here. We'll bring you something back."

She nodded.

The rest shifted to wolf form, and Noah led them out into the night.

SYDNEY WATCHED her mate lead the pack outside. It was just her and Shira's sister now. The girl was scared of her. She couldn't have been much more than nineteen. Still, it was surreal to Sydney that anyone should be scared of her. She'd always been the weak one that had to fear everybody else. The only reason she hadn't spent a lot of her life huddled in a corner was because her father had made it abundantly clear that if any harm came to her they would suffer a slow and painful death. And he'd acted on the threat more than once when she'd gotten minor injuries over the years.

A large animal pelt lay on the floor in front of a few chairs. Sydney picked it up and wrapped it around Livia. "Let's get you cleaned up. Where do you keep your first aid?" She was sure her blood would heal others now, but she wouldn't cross her mate or undermine him when he was trying to solidify his alpha status with the pack.

The girl relaxed a fraction and led Sydney to a small

room off to the side. Sydney cleaned the girl's wounds and bandaged her up, trying not to be squeamish about the fact that her mate had just done that.

"He could have killed me. It would have been completely normal," Livia said.

Sydney was rusty on how packs functioned, but deep down she knew that was right. Especially with this girl being Shira's sister. As brutal as it looked, that had been mercy. And from the expressions she'd seen on the faces of the pack, they had all read the signal loud and clear. Noah wasn't going to be pushed around, but he'd give them a chance to follow him.

"When you guys were being shown to your room last night, I told Shira she shouldn't have brought you here, but she wouldn't listen. She said Noah was too strong. She thought if she'd challenged him in the desert that he would have taken her out and taken the pack then and there. She said he hadn't marked you, and she was going to try to get him to mark her instead to get rid of you."

Sydney's hand went to her throat to touch the vicious-looking mark Noah had left there. "She wouldn't have had a chance. I've known Noah since we were children. We've always been destined for one another."

Sydney knew Shira couldn't have competed with a true mate no matter what her strategy was. Shira must not have believed it was true. It wasn't hard to see why. With Noah being strong enough to lead a pack, the idea that his true mate would be some weak little barely-a-vampire would be laughable to almost anyone. It had seemed unlikely even to Sydney until she'd felt the first effects of his blood.

8

N oah shifted back to his human form as he reached the shelter of the train station lobby. He'd have to maintain these displays of power for a while to remind them. He didn't want to have to do something truly vicious to keep himself and Sydney safe. He liked the pack and felt bad he'd taken their leader from them.

The pack had accepted him as their new leader so quickly, it reminded Noah what a fraud he was. Another wolf wouldn't have been so surprised. He kept looking for duplicity but couldn't find it in anyone.

He didn't understand packs, not really. He'd lived isolated, watching other wolves through glass, having brief conversations or mostly overhearing brief conversations among others in the exercise yard. There had been nothing of substance. No cohesion. No hierarchy.

There had been times when a wolf had tried to form a mini-pack during recreation hours in the yard, but the guards would quickly shut it down, isolating the would-be leader from others immediately with no hope of ever rejoining the group. It was a warning to the others about organizing. Most of them went mad with *no* interaction with others. Even the smallest interaction was better than nothing.

Noah might have been one of those would-be pseudo-alphas driven mad by total isolation, if not for the fact that he'd been taken so young. As a child, he couldn't lead anything, so he'd stayed out of everybody's way and observed the structure of how everyone had fit together at the facility. It had an organization to it, but it wasn't the same as how a pack worked. Not exactly.

Now he found himself surrounded by pack, wolves he had thought would be more a means to an end to safely get him to his family, but who now might become a second family. They'd bonded out in the desert. It felt natural and right. Running free and hunting was exhilarating. He'd barely been able to contain his excitement. All the new and exciting smells. The hunt, the kill. How had he survived at all without any of that?

Maybe it was unfair to judge them for submitting to his leadership so easily when he found just being with them out there in the wildness had melted much of his anti-social wall. He'd still need a lot of space and time to himself away from others, but they didn't make him uncomfortable like they had the first night.

One of the other wolves struggled just outside the door to reclaim his form. It was a wolf named Milo. Out in the desert, Noah had thought Milo might make a good second-in-command for the pack. His instincts were proving right on that score.

"Noah?" the wolf hesitated, testing the appropriateness of first names. But if Noah wanted this pack to trust him, he couldn't run things like an army all the time. There was a time for titles and a time for names.

"Yeah?"

"I thought you might want to see the transportation we're using when we leave." Milo tossed some sweatpants to him, and he put them on.

Noah followed him to the back of the train station. Behind two sets of tracks and one ancient train were several dozen motorcycles. He watched as Milo straddled one and cranked it up.

"Want to go for a ride?" The beta tossed him some keys. "That's Shira's bike."

It looked much the same as the others. They were all black and silver.

"Sure." He wasn't at all sure. "I've never ridden one before, though."

Milo goggled. "How is that possible?"

Time for a half-truth. "My pack growing up had access to some demon dimensional portals and we otherwise lived in a small area. We didn't use cars or trucks much, either." All of this was true. He was just conveniently leaving out the part about how he hadn't been properly socialized with others past the age of eight.

"It's pretty simple. Let me show you."

Noah was glad Milo was being cool about it. After everything else that had happened in the past twenty-four hours, being introduced to something new wasn't the highest crime in the world. But then he had second thoughts.

"Let's wait and do this tomorrow night after we hunt."

"Sure." He didn't ask why, and Noah wouldn't have told him, anyway. It was a sign that Milo accepted him as the new alpha, that he didn't pry or push for information not offered freely.

Noah had felt comfortable leaving one relatively weak female wolf alone with Sydney, especially after his mate had made a show of strength earlier, but he wasn't sure about leaving her alone with an entire pack.

As they made their way back to the front of the building, Noah turned to Milo. "I've been meaning to ask... are there no pups in this pack?" It had seemed odd to Noah when he'd seen all the wolves together the first time, but an opportunity to ask about it hadn't come up.

Milo's face went dark. "It's too dangerous. Livia is from the last generation of pups that were allowed. Shira was quite a bit older than her. Their parents died trying to protect her younger brother from some vampires. The boy died as well. Soon after that was when Shira took over and banned reproduction."

"Forever?" There wouldn't be any kids in his and Sydney's future. Sydney herself was an anomaly, but she was still a vampire, and female vampires couldn't have children. But he hadn't expected to lead a pup-free pack.

"Just until things got safer. But they never did. Now I think most everybody's okay with it. I mean, we do a lot of drinking and cavorting without clothing. Our den hasn't been child friendly since Shira's sister came of age.

I don't know if we could all comfortably adjust, so I'm not sure it'll be an issue."

"And what if there's an accident?" Noah pressed. Therian breeds in general were less fertile than humans, due to their much longer lifespans, and werewolves were more in tune with the times they were able to reproduce and the times they weren't, but accidents still weren't unheard of.

"Shira had a recipe for an herbal concoction to take care of it. It's only happened a couple of times, and the wolves involved were in agreement. The other option is to leave the pack. It's too dangerous for pups here. It's dangerous enough for the adults."

Noah nodded. He didn't disagree. The world wasn't the world he'd heard stories about as a pup. Resources were too scarce. And just the thought of another pup like him being taken captive by the human world and used for blood magic filled him with rage. It was bad enough to steal away the life of an adult who'd had a chance to live some of it, but there were parts of his life he would never have or get back, things that would always make him *other* from the rest of them who had normal childhood memories.

"Noah?"

He stopped and turned back to Milo.

"We all loved and respected Shira, but they're following you and acting like nothing happened because they need you. And we all saw it go down. She initiated the attack, and that was stupid. She let us down. It's not that the world is moving on and we don't care she's gone. It's that the rest of us are going to die if we don't work as a unit. We've seen a lot of tragedy, and we just want to survive it. If you can help us do that, you'll never have to worry about not counting on us."

Noah wasn't sure about all that, but the one thing he was sure about was that his new beta was sincere. There was no artifice there, no grand agenda. If he'd gotten one good thing genetically from his dad, it had been his instincts about people.

Noah clapped Milo on the shoulder. "I know. I was suspicious of intentions until I ran with them. For what it's worth, I didn't want it to go down like that, but she was going to kill me. I couldn't leave Sydney behind. What would have happened to her left alone with you guys?"

The beta didn't respond because they both knew. The pack would have ripped her to shreds and danced in the blood. That's if they didn't whore her around the group first. Relations with vampires was tense enough. They wouldn't have cared that Sydney wasn't their enemy, that she couldn't have hurt a fly last night. Now? The outcome of a confrontation with her was debatable.

Noah strode into the lobby to find the metal screaming out of the sound system again. The pack was more relaxed than they'd been since he was first introduced to them. A couple of wolves cuddled on one sofa in their wolf forms. Others ran around in human form.

All the clothes were in piles on the floor, and most appeared too lazy to sort through them to find their own. Noah's original pack wasn't as uptight about nudity as humans could be, but this pack took it to a whole other level.

Shouting rose from the bar. Noah rushed in to find a crowd around Sydney. He tensed, ready to rip heads off bodies.

"There is no way," one of the guys said.

Sydney laughed. "Oh yes there is."

As Noah moved closer, he could see five shots of the home brew whiskey lined up on the bar in front of his mate. Noah wasn't going to spoil it for her by giving away the fact that vampires metabolized alcohol faster than humans or even most therians. Strangely, drugs and alcohol affected them more strongly when it came through drunk or drugged human blood. Straight alcohol posed less of an issue. Being as close as his pack had been to Anthony and his vampires had given them a clearer picture into things than these wolves had been afforded.

It wasn't as if this pack would sit down with vampires for drinks to learn this sort of thing.

Noah was betting she'd never been able to do this before his blood—another fact he wasn't going to point out to spoil her fun. If this got her more accepted by the pack, as long as she didn't get hurt, he wasn't saying a thing.

Then she downed them. One right after the other. By the last one she smacked her hand on the bar about ten times just to cope with it. The werewolves around her all howled as if she'd just led them into successful battle.

"Told you!" Sydney shouted.

Noah cleared his throat and the group turned serious and moved out of his way. "Having fun?" he asked. And to think, he'd worried about her alone with them. Fate hadn't made a mistake when it had put them together.

She winked at him. "A blast. You?"

"It's not terrible," he admitted. But now that he knew she was okay, he needed space away from everyone. Quiet.

It was crazy. He could never tell anyone this, but he wished he was back in his cell because it was quiet and predictable and cozy in a completely fucked-up way. He wanted to be free. He wanted to be with Sydney and see his family and go back home and have a pack. He wanted all of the things that seemed to have been just laid at his feet overnight. But the noise, the unpredictability, the constant socialization was getting to him. And he wasn't sure how much longer he could wear the mask tonight.

He recalled loving these things as a pup, but now... he felt broken. It hadn't been so clearly apparent what was wrong with him, but something inside him had died in that place. Every day as he'd said his name to himself and every afternoon when he'd dreamed of the past, he'd thought he was holding onto everything, but it had all slipped through his fingers one granule at a time until he was left with this shell that needed to get away before he crawled out of his skin.

He pulled Sydney away from the group, far enough to be out of earshot. "Are you drunk?"

"A little," she admitted.

"Then I want you to come upstairs to the room with me. I know you're stronger now, and I think I have their loyalty, but it's too soon to know for sure. I don't want to leave you with them like this."

He half expected her to become belligerent. Her inhibitions were way down, and he still didn't completely trust the pack would respect him enough to not take advantage of that. But she didn't fight to stay behind with the others.

"Are you okay?" she asked, coming back to herself.

"Fine. I just need some space."

She was skeptical but didn't question him again in the bar.

"We're going upstairs," Noah said. "Don't disturb us unless there is an emergency. We'll see you tomorrow in the lobby at sunset. And start packing. As soon as the moon begins to wane, we have to get on the road and head home."

One of the wolves at the bar spoke up. "Are we going to join your family's pack?"

Noah shook his head. "No. We'll stay separate. There will be no integrating of the packs. We should be able to share general space, but it would be better if we remained our own group."

The wolf looked relieved. Noah didn't blame him. As much as he missed his family and their pack, and as much as he feared he couldn't handle the alpha thing, his instincts screamed differently. He didn't want to be in constant battle with his dad. They'd find a makeshift den separate from the hive.

He led Sydney from the group. As they left, the wolves got rowdy again, letting out howls because of course they assumed he and Sydney were going to their private den—or suite—for mating purposes.

It was a possibility, but more important to him was to

escape before he combusted from too much social interaction.

SYDNEY FOLLOWED Noah upstairs to what she'd been privately thinking of as the alpha suite. She still couldn't believe the wolves seemed so willing to leave their home. If this place weren't so far from her family and Noah's, and if it wasn't so close to the city, she'd want to stay. They had a cool set-up.

The irony of wanting to live close to her parents wasn't lost on her, but it wasn't as if she'd wanted to get away from them. She'd just wanted her own autonomy, and not to be treated like an over-sheltered teenager for the next several centuries. Hardly an unreasonable desire.

Tension rolled off her mate. From his perspective it might have been foolish of her to be in the bar, surrounded by werewolves and getting drunk. Though she was much stronger now, she wasn't silly enough to think she could take on the entire pack in a fight. She didn't even think Noah could do that if they collectively turned on him. Though he'd leave enough bodies on the ground to make the rest think twice before attempting that suicide mission.

Sydney had no idea what had come over her when that wolf openly defied her, insisting he wouldn't accept a vampire alpha. It was a rage that had risen from the depths of her being to flow out through her muscles as she shoved the wolf as far and as fast as she could. Her heart had pounded in her chest. She'd never escalated any interaction with anyone to violence because she knew she couldn't back it up.

She wanted to blame it on Noah's blood, something in werewolves that influenced her. That might be partly true, but it was also an impotent rage that had simmered in her for as long as she could remember. It had taken hold the night she'd woken to find she wasn't allowed to play with Noah anymore. It had grown stronger when she'd heard he'd disappeared. And it kept piling on with each restriction her father added to her life in the name of *protecting her.*

She knew he loved her and worried and wanted to keep her safe, but once she'd reached adulthood, shouldn't her fate have been in her own hands? The anger had grown so strong and so much a part of her that it had blended into the background, simmering underneath the facade of *Sweet Sydney*—the person they all thought she was.

Noah's blood wasn't new rage. It was permission. Agency. The ability to DO something. So when that wolf had implied as so many others around her had before, that she was less-than, it had been the final straw. She hadn't thought how it might negatively affect Noah. She hadn't considered it might incite fighting or put the two of them in danger. All she'd cared about was that she'd spent far too long being mild and meek and trying to push the rage down underneath the inability to express it.

She'd been shocked when the wolves had looked at her with new respect after that. It was only then that she remembered things she'd seen her father do to maintain his power and the bits of pack behavior she'd observed when she was a kid still playing with Noah. There was so much politics under the surface of any powerful person, so much artifice—a carefully controlled act and sleight of hand, dancing like a puppet to keep the others gaping up at you in wonder so they didn't turn on you.

After that moment, she'd realized they saw her as part of the new alpha pair—not some abnormally weak freak vampire that Noah had for some reason taken under his protection. She'd proven herself, and as long as she didn't back down from them or act nervous around them, they'd continue to see her this way. The shots at the bar had been pure politics. Part of her was grateful Noah had dragged her away, because she really was a bit drunk, and it might not enhance her new bad ass image to be stumbling all over the place.

Noah pulled her into their room and locked and barricaded the door.

"Are you upset with me?"

In response, he shoved her against the wall, his lips pressed against hers. His mouth trailed to her throat to place kisses there as well. "Why would I be upset with you?" he rumbled. "The pack loves you. They like you more than they like me."

"Does that bother you?"

His mood changed like a switch had been flipped. She'd thought they were about to do exactly what the wolves downstairs thought he'd dragged her away for, but now he seemed different, his own mask slipping. He sat on the edge of the bed and put his head in his hands.

Sydney stood there for a minute, not sure if he wanted comfort or space or what to do for him. She'd obviously said something wrong. Maybe he was angry or jealous. The pack had already bonded with him somewhat, but they still weren't at the drinking buddy stage, something she'd managed in about fifteen minutes when they'd returned from the hunt.

He looked up, and everything fell away. The image he'd erected to protect her and get them safely back home was gone, and in its place, he was just that little boy again. Fiercely protective of her, but just some guy. Not the technological savant who'd orchestrated their escape. Not the superhero who'd slaughtered humans and werewolves to keep her safe. Not the alpha. Just the man.

He sighed. "No, Sydney. It doesn't bother me. I'm relieved they like you, and that you're sociable enough to keep the pressure off me. I don't know how to be around people. They're going to figure me out."

She sat beside him on the bed, leaning her cheek against his shoulder. "They don't know your history. And even if they did, if you are strong enough to lead them, what does it matter? You escaped a near-impossible-to-escape place that was well-guarded."

Noah shrugged. "They had holes in their security. Big holes. That was luck. If it hadn't been for that, I never could have gotten us out, even with the unnatural strength I had on my side last night."

"It wasn't luck. Everything came together for us. It was all meant to be."

"You sound like the seers."

The cities had a lot of those. Cary Town, not so much anymore.

Then Noah broke down for real. All that he'd held in —possibly for years—all that he'd been through the past few nights came flowing out of him. Sydney held him and let him get it out. She hadn't been in that place for very long, thanks to Noah.

She tried not to think about what would have happened if he hadn't been there. She would have had no hope. She never would have been strong. She would have spent the rest of her days in that sterile cube and out in the exercise yard trying to fade into the background so some random therian or vampire didn't kill her simply for existing as something weaker than them.

Even if she managed to survive that, deep down she'd known they hadn't intended to keep her long. She was a curiosity. Perhaps they wanted to use her blood in experiments to determine how it might benefit them, but in the long run there was little she could offer that couldn't be gotten from any other vampire, and her blood didn't infuse magic with extra power like therian blood did. There would have been no reason to keep her alive.

The experiments with the UV light lasers had confirmed it. If she'd died in all that? Well, who cared? They were merely curious, and curiosities didn't last long in this world.

Sydney closed her eyes, trying to stop seeing Jacob's lifeless face. Yes, he'd betrayed her. He'd deserved to die at her fangs, but not under those conditions. It had felt all wrong. But her few days of fear and captivity only put a finer point on Noah's.

What had he gone through? Not just seeing her like that in there, but what had they done to him for all those years? Even if they'd only ever kept him captive and drawn blood every day for use in their magic, it was still beyond cruel to keep a wolf in a small enclosure like that, to prevent him from being socialized properly and from having a pack.

"Noah?"

"Yeah?"

She wasn't sure if him crying in front of her was because macho hadn't been properly socialized into him, or if it was because she was his mate, and he trusted her that much. She had to believe it was the latter because of the mask he'd worn while captive and again now with the pack to keep things under control. He wasn't stupid. He'd known how he had to be in order to stay alive both on the inside and on the outside of those walls.

"I might be able to help with some of this stuff you're dealing with. Maybe I could soften the edges," she said.

"How?"

Sydney hesitated. She'd never manipulated emotions before. It wasn't a skill she'd had. But now, with Noah's blood and all the changes that had taken place, if she was truly a *real vampire* now, as his mate, she could help him. Her lack of hypnotic abilities had been connected to all the other weaknesses she'd inherited from the accident of her unnatural birth. It was as if she were a battery that just hadn't had enough juice to get and stay going. But now she did, and every door that had previously been closed to her stood wide open.

"It's this mental connection thing. Vampires can do it

with humans when they feed normally to some extent, but it's especially strong with mates. The emotion part, anyway. Vampires can't get into their mates' thoughts, but we can help with emotion. I can't make any of it not have happened, but I can help you get through it."

In reality, while she she couldn't read his thoughts, as his mate she could implant new, happier memories. But she knew he wouldn't want that—to never know what was real or fake inside his head. Taking the worst of the sting from his history would have to be enough.

"Okay." Noah held out his arm.

She didn't ask why he didn't offer his throat. There were limits to everything, and maybe that was too much intimacy for what she was about to do. Maybe he wanted to keep that as something associated with other things.

Sydney bit into the offered arm and tasted all the anguish he'd tried to keep locked away from her. All the self-doubt and insecurity. Those stupid fucking bastards. She wanted to go back in and kill every single one of them that Noah hadn't gotten to. She wanted to rip down their shiny city and leave it in ruins, like they'd left vampire and therian societies in ruins, like they'd left lives in ruins—including Noah's.

She thought about his parents mourning him, about her parents mourning her. She thought about everything Noah had lost even in spite of all he'd recently gained and would have returned to him. She thought about all of these things, and as she drank she let those thoughts go and focused only on sending him peace and warmth and security—all the things he probably couldn't even remember having.

She melted against him as his free hand ran through her hair, and she started to cry as if his pain was transferring into her. And maybe it was. Only it was more distant and detached because it hadn't actually happened to her. Still, the emotion swamped her.

"Stop, Sydney. This is hurting you."

Big stupid wolf. Of course it hurt her. But it would hurt her no matter what. If she had no power to help him, it would just be the same powerless uselessness she'd lived with for nearly three decades already. It would be a slow-burning pain as she watched him unravel from the pressure of trying to be all the things to everyone that he'd never been properly taught to be.

When she'd taken the worst of what was on the surface and replaced it with something better, she pulled away from him. "I'm not letting my mate suffer in silence pointlessly. What have you got to prove? After all the years you were in there and everything you risked to get us out? You told them all that I was their alpha, too. If that's true, let me take on part of this."

After a long time, he nodded. "I just don't want to cause you pain."

"You gave me strength. Let me give you some peace."

"When you put it like that, it sounds completely reasonable," he said.

They held each other for a long time just breathing each other in, and then somehow their matching breaths turned into caressing and kissing, and then they were two entwined naked bodies making love.

"I can't believe this is only your second time doing this," she said.

Noah growled. "Hey!" But he wasn't mad.

They spent the next couple of hours alternately exploring each other's bodies and snuggling together in the bed.

He nipped over his mark as his hand slid down between her legs for what felt like the thousandth time that night. "We're going to have to move the bedding back into the bathroom before the sun comes up."

Sydney groaned and stretched. "That's still so many hours away. And I can't move. I think you broke me."

He laughed. A real laugh. "Somehow I doubt that." A beat passed, then he went very still.

"Noah?"

He raised a hand to silence her, then he got up and prowled to the door. He poked his head into the hallway, then came back inside. "Sydney, I need your help."

She jumped up, thinking there was danger. But when she reached him, she saw the problem. It wasn't danger. Outside in the hallway were freshly killed rabbits, wine that looked to be several decades old—probably from before the wars—and clothes for Noah. Most likely cobbled together from other pack members.

"I need to learn how to ride a motorcycle," he said.

"Okay. I have no idea what that has to do with the pack paying tribute but..."

Sydney gathered up the clothes and wine, while Noah brought the rabbits inside.

"I was just thinking that I feel better, and I think I can handle it tonight. I wanted to know if you wanted to go with me."

"Definitely."

Noah shifted into his wolf form and demolished the rabbits in short order. Then he pounced on her and licked the side of her face like he had when they were kids and all she'd known was the wolf.

"Ewww, gross, Noah! Get off me. You have rabbit breath!"

He licked her one more time, then shifted back to his human form. "I'm going to grab a shower before we go. Come with me."

"My legs don't hold me up anymore."

"I'll hold you up."

9

Sydney blushed when she and Noah reached the bar, and the wolves started howling at them. She didn't think his original intent for taking her upstairs had been sex, but it had been the pack's assumption. And she knew they smelled like it. Werewolf noses didn't lie.

She stuck close to Noah because she didn't want to be pulled away by the females for gossip. Their jealousy was barely contained. It had been much easier to gain acceptance with the male members of the pack. She wasn't taking some spot they'd fantasized about having in the hierarchy. But the bitches could get over it because it wasn't as if Noah had been a longstanding member. They'd just met the guy.

"Are you okay?" Noah asked.

"Yeah, why?" She looked up to find several of the wolves had taken several steps back.

"You're growling. You look ready to attack."

"Oh. Sorry. I was thinking."

Noah went back to speaking with Milo. Sydney hadn't heard an official announcement, but the pack had either been informed through gossip, or they'd simply intuited that Milo was the new beta. Or maybe he'd been Shira's beta as well.

Noah's feelings about trying to run a pack with his history were beginning to seem logical. How were a wolf who hadn't been properly socialized in a pack for most of his life and a vampire going to successfully run a whole pack?

"Why can't we just leave tonight?" the beta asked.

Noah pulled Milo and Sydney farther away from the others. "Motorcycle lesson?"

"Well, yeah, but I meant after that. Or tomorrow night. We could leave tomorrow night."

Noah growled. "Why are you in such a hurry to leave your home?"

The beta glanced around to see if anyone was eavesdropping, then he turned back to Noah and Sydney. "I didn't want to say anything, but the night Shira brought you guys here, one of our wolves didn't come back from the hunt. He could have been killed by a vampire or in the fight when they were creating a diversion so you guys could get away, but he also could have been taken. We haven't found a body. If they captured him, we're sitting ducks. The den isn't safe anymore. We have to leave."

In Sydney's opinion, this den had never been particularly safe. It was too close to the established city for her taste. She could understand why the vampires would troll outside the cities, waiting for a human to disobey the grand order and be thrown out to the monsters. But why wolves?

Unless the wolves were sometimes feeding on humans themselves.

"Why have you guys been this close to the city to begin with?" Sydney asked.

"We had an uneasy alliance with the vampires," Milo said, "to keep more from being kidnapped. Some of us suspected Shira might have had a thing with their leader. Once they know she's gone, our alliance might be gone with it. It may be why she didn't take a mate from among the pack."

Or she didn't want to give her power away. But Sydney kept that thought to herself. They may have accepted Shira as the sole alpha as long as she was single, and as long as one of them might have a chance at alpha by becoming her mate, but the second she took someone, things would change. Wasn't that how it had always been through history? Sydney hadn't known her long, but Shira seemed like the type who enjoyed her power and wanted to maintain it. Not that Sydney could blame her. Power became quickly addictive. If told she could keep Noah but lose her strength or keep her strength but lose Noah, she'd choose Noah, but it wouldn't be easy.

"You wouldn't need so much protecting if you were farther from the city. This is still inside the radius of where they would go to take werewolves and other therians," Noah said.

The vein in his neck had become more prominent as his muscles tensed. Sydney tried to ignore it. It would hardly be appropriate for her to launch herself at him and feed right now. Anyway, she'd just eaten.

"But being close to the city has its advantages. We can leech off their power grid and use the water infrastructure already in place. In case you weren't aware, life is easier with hot running water and lights."

Noah gave him a warning growl and Milo quickly remembered who he was speaking to.

"Sorry, sir. My mouth got away from me."

"How many wolves can reclaim their human form under the full moon?" Noah asked.

"Only a couple of others besides myself. And of course, Shira could."

"That's why we aren't leaving yet. Travel as a group would be impossible."

The Beta glanced over at Sydney, a touch of resentment in his eyes. They'd have to ditch the motorcycles and any belongings they might otherwise want to take with them if they went now, but they could run as a pack of wolves if it weren't for her.

Sydney growled.

"You know it's true. A vampire in the pack makes it impossible for us to leave during a full moon."

"You're right. This is too complicated," Noah said. "I'll just take my mate and leave."

Milo looked panicked and a few of the other wolves ambled over. "NO! You can't leave us."

So they'd been listening the whole time. Great. Noah must not have moved them far enough away from the others.

The wolf that had spoken said, "Look, we'll work it

out. It's not ideal, but we like Sydney. She's pretty cool. If she's part of the deal, okay, but we need you."

It seemed that a few of the wolves weren't entirely sold on Sydney's *coolness*.

"Oh yeah?" Noah said. "Well, let me educate you about the truth of the pack alpha you need so badly. I was kidnapped by those *people* and separated from my pack when I was just a pup. I was their captive for two decades before I got out. The only reason I escaped was because they had flaws in their security system, it was my twenty-eighth birth moon, and Sydney got captured. So I am not an alpha by any definition of that word. I can't lead you. I have only the slightest fucking clue how packs even work. I've been bullshitting my way through it this entire time. So there's your alpha pair. A vampire, and a wolf that doesn't know how to be a wolf. Come on Sydney, we're leaving."

He grabbed her arm and took her out of the bar.

"It'll be safer to travel with a pack," Sydney said as he dragged her through the lobby like some errant child.

He growled, and fur began to sprout out of his arms. She'd never seen him this angry before. They were halfway through the lobby when the revolving doors opened and in poured human magic users from the city. Their ringleader held a roughed-up looking guy who'd been beaten nearly to death.

"Oscar!" Livia shouted.

The missing pack wolf. But if he was a werewolf, why wasn't he healing? The pack might not have had a strong enough wolf to lead them all, but they were *still* werewolves. Sydney suspected magic had been incorporated in the wolf's torture to overcome any healing advantage.

The human threw the missing wolf to the ground.

"I'm sorry," he said. "I tried not to tell them. W-where's Shira?"

Noah began barking orders to the others to shift. "Sydney, take this guy to the bar out of the way. I don't want you in the middle of this."

She wanted to argue, but it wasn't as if they could get away now without a fight, and she didn't want to risk her mate by distracting him. With her claim, it was unlikely he'd die. And she'd keep telling herself that over and over to get through this because every instinct inside her screamed not to leave his side.

Sydney helped the wounded werewolf up. The violence started all too fast, exploding in the lobby like a bomb that had just ticked down and detonated. There was no warning, just a flurry of fur and growling and magic sizzling the air. A stray ball of magical electricity hit her on the back as she took Oscar out of the lobby and into the bar.

Someone cranked the sound system way up. The metal pounding out was nearly deafening. It drowned out the jazz in the bar.

"Where's Shira?" Oscar asked again over the din.

Sydney took him to the back lounge area as far away from the noise as she could get him, trying desperately not to think about Noah out there. She wanted to kill the wolf that had led the humans back to the den, but then she remembered the UV lasers.

It hadn't taken long for her to break and kill Jacob,

and these people had a pack member for over twenty-four hours. She doubted he'd slept in that time.

"What happened to Shira?" But from the look on his face, he knew.

"Shira is dead. My mate and I are the new alphas." It seemed so cold to state so bluntly when Oscar's people... when her mate could be dying out there, but if she thought too hard about the chaos happening in the lobby, she wouldn't get through these next moments.

Oscar growled. Given his condition, it wasn't a very menacing growl, but he made an effort. "You're a vampire."

Sydney smiled, but it didn't reach her eyes. "Great species identification. Now let's move on to shapes and colors!" The sarcasm was inappropriate right now. She knew that, but the fear of her mate dying or of both of them being dragged back to the place they'd only just escaped, sat like a heavy weight trying to press her down beneath the earth and suffocate her.

"I'm a dead man. They should have just killed me. I might have had a chance if Shira was here."

Livia rushed into the bar. She looked worse for wear. The bandage Sydney put on her earlier in the night had all but come off. So much for that.

"Oscar! I thought you were dead." She crushed him in a hug, and he groaned.

"Not yet," he said, giving Sydney a look as if she were going to order his execution.

That was Noah's department, not hers. And given how a few minutes ago he'd been ready to abandon them, Sydney wasn't sure it was right for him to order anybody's head on a platter.

"Oh screw this," Sydney said. She ripped into her wrist and held it out to Oscar.

"No, way."

She growled. "Drink!"

He looked briefly at Livia who nodded quickly. So he drank. Oscar healed before her eyes, and then she turned her attention to the female wolf.

"But what about the punishment earlier?"

"I don't care. There are bigger things to worry about. You both need to be able to fight. I'll deal with Noah if he has a problem with it. Drink."

It didn't take much blood to help both wolves reclaim their healing abilities.

"Why is that music so fucking loud?" Sydney asked. It was so irritating, it made her teeth grind. Now seemed like a stupid time to turn the lobby into a rave.

"It's a magical defense system," Livia said. "It doesn't stop those electricity balls they throw, but it keeps them from chanting and having more of an advantage. The louder it is, the better it works. Shira got it a few years ago from some witch who was passing through. What was her name? Frances? Fontaine?"

"Fiona," Oscar offered.

"Right! Fiona. She was traveling with a panther therian and she gave us the music in exchange for shelter for a few days. There is no way we would have trusted she wasn't working for the city. But she had a therian mate, so it seemed pretty unlikely."

The music stopped suddenly. Sydney ran into the

lobby, followed by Oscar and Livia. The humans were all dead, along with half a dozen of the pack. More were seriously wounded.

"We need to get out of here, now," Noah said. "When the magic users don't return by morning, they'll send more. Everyone pack light and put your bags with your bikes. We'll find somewhere nearby we can hole up in until the full moon passes. We can move the bikes there during the day while Sydney is resting."

Several of the wolves who weren't too badly injured moved to carry out the order, but a few stood defiantly in the middle of the lobby.

"You were right," one of them said. "Just go. You've brought nothing but chaos with you since you got here. You don't want us, anyway. We can't go anywhere tonight. Some are too injured to be moved. So I guess we're targets until they heal. Thanks."

"Fine," Noah said. "Sydney..."

Sydney walked to the center of the lobby with Oscar and Livia behind her. It didn't escape the pack's notice that the wolves were fully healed.

"Noah, can I speak with you privately?"

He growled but followed her out the back door and far enough away this time that no one could overhear.

"You gave them your blood didn't you? I can't believe that you would..."

"Noah, shut up."

He looked angry and then hurt, and then angry again.

"I'm sorry. I shouldn't have said that. You are kidding yourself. You *are* an alpha. You took control in there when the magic users came. Yes, there were casualties, but no one would have survived without you, and they all know that whether they are ready to admit it or not. The humans would have won and taken those they didn't kill captive."

Noah's jaw clenched. "They don't want me. They don't want you."

"Give them time. They loved Shira. You need a pack. You know you do, and you're not going to be content to integrate into your dad's pack. You need your own people. This is them. If you think fate brought me to you, maybe it brought us to them, too. I can get every single one of them on our side if you give me a chance."

Noah pulled her to him and held her. "You're right. I know what you're going to do. At least feed again first."

Sydney drank long and deep, no longer afraid to absorb that kind of power because she needed it to help lead this pack. And they needed her. She wouldn't continue to be afraid and back away from something she needed to make her strong.

She turned and started back for the door.

"Hey Sydney?"

"Yeah?"

"You know I love you, right? It's not just fate and blood. I've loved you since we were kids."

"Noah. Dammit, don't make me all weepy before I have to go in there and be a bad ass."

He chuckled.

"I love you, too."

The room was still tense when they returned to the lobby.

"I'm going to make the same offer I made last night," Noah said. "Anyone who wants to stay behind can stay behind. Anyone who wants to come with us can come with us."

"Didn't you say you didn't want us?" one of the wolves asked, sounding bitter and hurt.

"Didn't I also say I was kept captive for years? I'm not going to be perfect, but I won't threaten to abandon any of you again. I swear it."

"What about Oscar? What will happen to him if we follow you?" Livia asked. She gripped his arm as if it were a lifeline holding her stable out at sea.

Sydney hoped with every fiber of her being that Noah would make the right call on this one.

"Nothing will happen to Oscar. Do you guys not understand when I tell you I was their captive for years? I've watched them torture. I've watched them kill. I escaped most of it by being quiet and not looking threatening. The only thing they wanted from me was my blood. But when they want anything else from someone, it's much worse. Oscar can choose just like the rest of you. No grudges. No punishments. No killing."

Sydney moved through the group of wounded werewolves and fed them each her blood until they began to heal.

As the wolves healed, Noah moved to one side of the room. "Sydney and I will commit fully to you if you commit fully to us. If you're going with us, join me on this side of the lobby."

One by one the wolves came to stand with Noah until

the only wolves not standing with him were the ones that were dead.

NOAH WATCHED as the wolves joined him on his side of the room. He'd half-believed they would reject him now that they knew the truth of things. He'd been a fool to ever think it would remain a secret forever. When he'd been ready to run, it didn't seem to matter that they knew. It felt like the last word in an argument. *Look how stupid you were to follow me. You don't even know anything about me.*

The beta stepped forward. "Noah, sir, You want that motorcycle lesson now?"

He glanced at the other wolves to see if any were laughing at him, but they were all deadly solemn.

"Yeah, that would be good." He turned back to the pack. When he'd seen the motorcycles the previous night, he'd noticed they all had saddlebags on the sides. "Guys, pack whatever is necessary that you can fit on or inside your bike. We'll scout out a place tonight and get Sydney settled before sunrise, you can follow the scent when the sun comes up."

This time the wolves scattered to carry out the order. Some of them looked distraught. He didn't blame them. In the space of twenty-four hours they'd lost their leader, several other wolves, and now their home. He had no idea why they would follow him after all of that, but if the vampire alliance had broken down now and the humans knew the location of the den, it wouldn't be long until a lot more danger was on their doorstep. They had to move fast.

Sydney didn't say anything as they went to their room. Milo followed.

"Saddlebags for Shira's bike are in her closet. Sydney can use that. I'll get you some others from one of the fallen wolves"

"Thanks."

The beta started to leave.

"Hey, Milo. Tell them after they pack, they can bury those that died."

"They'll appreciate that."

Noah sat on the edge of the bed and watched while Sydney went through the clothes to find the few she could take. Possibly the only good thing about this was that they could all travel light. They had weapons already: fangs, claws, brute strength. They *were* weapons. Even Sydney, now.

They hunted, so they didn't need to pack food. Just clothing. And in truth, in a worst case situation they could simply live as wolves in the woods. It wouldn't be the first pack that had tried to blend as animals in that way to avoid the humans, but it didn't always work. Some of Noah's fellow prisoners had come from packs using that strategy. Their magical signature followed them wherever they went. Too close to a city or a strong magic user, and it was only a matter of time before they were found out.

Milo returned with saddlebags for Noah. "I'll wait downstairs for you guys."

When the door shut, Noah went through the clothing

the pack had brought him and tried everything on to determine what would fit best, what he could move and fight in if necessary and then put the chosen items into the bags.

"You're awfully quiet," he said. Sydney hadn't spoken a word since they'd left the lobby.

"I'm just thinking. I feel bad about everything they're leaving behind."

"They're taking their lives. It's leave and live or stay and die."

"We don't know they'll live. We don't know we will."

"I know we will." Fate couldn't be that cruel to bring her to him against all odds only to take her away again. He wouldn't allow it to happen.

When they were packed, Sydney gave the room one last look. "I kind of liked this place. Even though I knew we were never staying."

Noah led her down through the lobby one more time. The metal was playing again. Milo had been kind enough to explain immediately after the fighting why that music played and why it had been so loud.

He would have been angry when the music had gone up to piercing decibels, but the beat had energized him, made him faster, caused him to fight harder.

"Someone pack that music," he shouted as they headed toward the back door.

"On it!" Rafe shouted.

Milo stood beside outside next to the bikes.

The beta got on one of them and tossed a set of keys to Noah for the one beside him.

"And what about me?" Sydney asked.

"I thought you'd just want to ride with Noah."

"You thought wrong."

Noah laughed and shrugged. "You may as well teach us both at the same time." In truth, he was grateful she wanted to learn. It would make him feel less awkward learning something he should have been able to do when he was fourteen—and would have been able to do if not for being imprisoned.

Milo turned to Sydney, "Would they have any idea where you might be going? Where home is?"

She looked like a spooked animal. "I was betrayed by someone, and they knew where we were from. What if they're waiting for us when we get home? They'll know we can't travel during the day. What if they attack our families?"

"Don't they have wards and protections?" Milo asked.

"Yes, but they tried to keep magic and technology usage to a minimum to stay off the grid so as not to attract the humans. I don't know how heavy their security is, how many people the city would send, and if they can defend against it. Stupid sunlight! I wish I wasn't a vampire."

"We've got about five hours until sunrise. We need to get on the road and travel as far as we can," Milo said. "Then I'll go back and meet the others halfway to make sure they followed the trail. Where we heading?"

"Do you know where Cary Town is?" Sydney asked.

The beta laughed. "Do I know where Cary Town is? Everybody knows about Cary Town.

"Yes, but do you know *where* it is?"

"General vicinity. From there I'm sure you can tell me."

Sydney looked doubtful. "I only left once. I was running away. My dad can be overbearing and overprotective."

"You mean your sire?"

"No, my dad. I was born, not turned."

Milo's eyes widened. "Your dad isn't Anthony Burgess is he?"

"That's him."

"We had the vampire princess with us this whole time, and we didn't know it. The pack probably wouldn't have complained about a vampire alpha if they knew your lineage. Vampire or not, royalty is still royalty. It wouldn't feel shameful, at least."

"It's not as regal as you might think these days. Cary Town has broken down. There's just him, my mom, and a few other vampires and human mates they've captured over the years. Noah's old pack is there. There's a cranky old sorcerer and a werecat in the woods. And some vampire that doesn't talk much to my dad, but he lives with a guardian in the abandoned church. And that's Cary Town now. Otherwise it's a ghost town. Hardly worth visiting."

"Are there lots of wild places to run?"

"Yeah, I guess. I haven't been out very much."

Her description made Noah miss home. He still remembered the smell of the woods. He'd been too young to realize yet how much the world was changing for the worst and all the things he was about to lose. But no matter how deserted Cary Town had become, he couldn't imagine the caves his dad's pack lived in had changed much. Or the woods for that matter. The more deserted it was, the better, in his opinion.

"We need to get on the road," Noah said. "I'm sure when we get close I'll pick up a familiar scent."

Milo gave them a crash course in motorcycles. After a few false starts and one minor crash, they took off and rode for hours. Noah followed Milo until he was more confident with the bike. Then he took the lead. With one long stretch of deserted highway it was no great mystery which direction to go.

After a considerable time on the road, Sydney pulled out ahead and over to the shoulder. Noah and the beta came to a stop beside her.

"Is something wrong?" Noah asked.

"I can feel the sun coming soon. It's hard to explain. I didn't feel this way before because I was always too tired to notice. We need to start looking for a place for me to sleep for the day. There was a deserted farmhouse we stayed in on the trip down, I don't think it's very far from here."

"We'll follow if you want to try to look for it," Noah said.

Sydney nodded and started her bike back up. They followed her several miles until she took an exit and went down more deserted road. And then, looming in front of them, was the farmhouse surrounded by acres and acres of land with some woods behind it. Great, he could hunt something before they had to get back on the road again.

They pulled their bikes into a dilapidated barn.

"I'm going to head back to meet the others," Milo said.

"Okay." Noah watched Milo disappear down the road, then he followed Sydney into the farmhouse, his senses on high alert for any other squatters. But it was deserted just like she'd said.

10

S ydney was beginning to question her own judgment. What madness had overtaken her to make her think this was a good idea after the last time she'd been here?

But she knew the place. It was secure enough. And if Noah slept on the bed, he had a view outside the large picture window. No one could sneak up on them here.

"Sydney? You okay?"

"It's hard to be here."

"Did you know he planned to turn you over to them when you were here the last time?"

She nodded, staring at the closet as if it might come to life and devour her. "It's just... not good memories. And it makes me think about him, and then I remember killing him. I wish there had been another place, but I knew this was safe."

Noah pulled her to him and held her close. "You're safe with me."

Of course she was safe with him. She'd never once doubted it. Not since she'd known who he was, at least. Before that it had been iffy.

Given his captivity, maybe someone else would have doubted him, worried that place had changed him and made him dangerous. But the way he looked at her and protected her now was the same as when they'd been kids. Whatever had changed in him, that was one thing that remained constant.

The red glow of the sun started to peek over the horizon. She'd felt dawn screaming inside her brain louder and louder, but she'd ignored it while trying to deal with the farmhouse. She had to tell herself repeatedly that she wasn't crazy. This place was a known element, and they hadn't had time to be picky with sunrise breathing down their necks.

She jumped into the closet before the first ray of light could touch her skin.

"Sydney?"

"Yeah?"

"Is this going to be a safety risk every day? You leaping out of the way of the sun at the last minute?"

She managed a weak laugh. "No. I felt it coming for a while. I was just being a spaz. I'll listen to the yelling in my brain more next time."

"Good to hear."

The springs of the bed depressed as Noah sat down. His boots hit the floor, and then she heard the whisper of clothing that followed. When the sun got higher, she'd have no choice but to sleep, but she wished she could be out there snuggled with him. A couple of minutes later, a furry wolf body curled up next to her.

"Do you think we'll ever sleep with you in your human form?"

Not that she was complaining. It felt safe and peaceful and made her nostalgic for simpler times when she hadn't yet understood how dangerous the world was. As a child she'd woken many times with the wolf beside her.

Noah would play in the sun during the day with his friends, but he'd always be right there next to her after sunset.

He snorted in reply. Soon after, the power of the sun claimed the last of her energy for the day.

When Sydney woke, Noah was still curled around her snoring and twitching, deep in a dream. He'd no doubt become as nocturnal as she was from the way they'd scheduled his sleep and active times during his captivity.

She stayed in the dark closet, afraid the sun might still be up. After several minutes, she poked Noah in the side. He growled, nipped her lightly, then laid back down.

Sydney jabbed him harder. "Noah, wake up. I need you to check and see if the sun is down yet." Like she wanted to stay in this awful closet a minute longer than was necessary.

He grew more alert and went to check things out. A few minutes later, a naked Noah stood with the closet door open.

"It's safe. Sun's down."

Well, she could see that now with the door open.

He helped her up. She hated this closet. It had a weird smell she couldn't decipher and didn't want to think too much about. She worried some dead thing was buried beneath piles of moth-eaten clothing in the corner.

It had been deserted for ages, and she hated the idea of mice and other assorted creatures crawling over her as she slept. Only one more night until the moon would begin to wane, then hopefully she'd be sleeping for the rest of her days in a nice normal bed.

Sydney licked her lips at the sight of him. "When will the pack be here?"

"They're here already. They're on the other end of the house."

It was wise that they'd stayed so far from her and Noah. She couldn't imagine he'd be very sane and rational if he scented or sensed someone near his mate when she was so vulnerable.

"Can they hear us?"

"Probably."

"Oh." There went that idea.

But Noah didn't seem as upset by the potential for eavesdropping as she did. "They'll get over it," he said.

"But... I don't think..."

His eyes flashed gold. "You'll get over it, too. Besides, you need to feed."

Noah had removed most of her clothing when she put a hand over his. "I can't with them in here."

Annoyance flitted over his features, and he disappeared down the hallway. Sydney didn't care. Let him pout if that was how he was going to be about it. He might be just fine screwing with a bunch of people within hearing range, but she wasn't. She wasn't even sure if her aversion was normal for a vampire. It definitely wasn't for a wolf.

He returned several minutes later. "They're gone. I told them to go outside and hunt without me. They'll be too pre-occupied running to care what we're doing in here."

She was still irritated, but when he pulled her against him and his warm body pressed against hers, her irritation started to melt. As he trailed kisses down the side of her throat and over her breasts, it melted a bit more. And when he pushed her back on that awful old bed whose history she didn't even want to guess about, she didn't care anymore.

Noah nudged her legs apart, and she gasped when he drove into her. He stilled, cradling her in his arms. "Am I hurting you?"

"No, I'm okay. You're just so warm, it's always a shock."

"Eh, a few hundred years, you'll be fine," he joked.

Sydney giggled. When he got within range of her fangs, he nuzzled the mark he'd left on her throat. She turned her head and bit over the claim she'd left on him. A growl erupted from his throat.

She smiled against his skin. This time when she fed, she tasted something new. Contentment. Happiness. Love. When he reached orgasm, the taste of his blood grew richer, and it triggered her own release.

Afterward, they laid tangled together, neither eager to go anywhere.

"The old train station was a lot nicer," Noah commented.

"Yeah, well you were the one who just *had* to do it now."

Noah rolled his eyes, and got up. "You would have fed and jumped me like a crazy animal. You know you would have."

Sydney took in the view as he turned away and stretched. That perfect olive skin, muscles rippling as he moved. Yeah, she would have.

The only thing that marred his perfection was that stupid black number tattooed into his upper arm.

"I'm so angry those monsters put a number on you, like you were some thing they were tagging and keeping in a box."

"I *was* some thing they were tagging and keeping in a box," he said, staring out the window. The moon suddenly moved out from behind the clouds and Noah leapt out of the way of the light.

"Are you okay?" she asked.

"Yeah. I'm just not sure if I'll shift when the moon hits me if I haven't eaten first. It's still a full moon. I have less control right now."

"No. I mean... from everything."

He glanced down at the number on his arm. "Sydney, if you're talking about this, I'd planned to cover it with another tattoo when I got out. Most pack leaders have one, anyway."

Sydney hadn't realized at the time that Shira's snake

tattoo held any significance beyond her just wanting to look like a bad ass. But none of the other wolves had any tattoos that she'd noticed.

"Only an alpha can have tattoos on their arms. It's how visiting wolves know immediately who's in charge. It's been a tradition in wolf packs for hundreds of years."

"If you'd always planned to get a tattoo to cover the number, does that mean you always planned to lead a pack?"

Noah shrugged. "I figured I could get away with it in my dad's pack. It's not like he'd kill me for it, and he'd understand why I did it. And if I couldn't handle living with them without being in charge, I thought I could just be a lone wolf. I assumed that might happen, anyway. The tattoo thing is a pack law in most packs. If you're not in a pack, it's not an issue. In the end it means a wolf that becomes an alpha either has to stay an alpha, die in a challenge fight, or become a lone wolf. Once you take on that mantle of leadership, you can't ever follow inside another pack again. It's a big responsibility."

A rock hit the window. "Get dressed and meet me outside," Noah said. He'd shifted to alpha mode. She didn't much care for him barking orders at her, but he was under too much pressure to start a petty fight right now.

And yet... "So you can run around like that but I can't?" Sydney asked.

"Or be naked. I don't care. I assumed that would be an issue for you."

He assumed right. Noah disappeared again down the hallway, and Sydney started for her clothes. But then she stopped. He thought she was some prissy little vampire princess who couldn't handle public nudity. He was one hundred percent right about that, but once the stubbornness took hold, the logic went away, and she'd be damned if she'd prove him right.

She let out a growl and said, "Screw it."

11

Noah was surprised when he didn't immediately shift under the full moon. It was the first opportunity he'd had to test how he reacted to a regular full moon on an empty stomach. The blood moon had only been for the first night. Tonight it was a regular yellowish-white light hanging in the sky.

With Sydney having fed and weakening him, he'd been sure he would change to his wolf form. But he hadn't. The moon urged him to, tempting and teasing him with the warmth that felt like sunlight. The wind whispered to him to run and hunt. He smelled and heard rabbits scurrying away in the fields.

Milo waited for him outside the bedroom window.

"Hey, I'm sorry if I interrupted something in there," he said, now sheepish about the rock throwing.

"You didn't. I would have ignored you."

The beta chuckled uncomfortably. "I just wanted to

let you know we found a lake to bathe in if you want to get Sydney—"

"Let me stop you there. There is no way Sydney will be up for public bathing."

"Somebody talking about me?"

Noah spun to find his mate without a stitch of clothing, an impish grin on her face.

"Hey Sydney, there's a lake about a mile south of here if you want to clean up," Milo said.

"Oh yes, that sounds wonderful."

He arched a brow at Noah as Sydney blurred in the direction he pointed. "I think you underestimate her," he said.

"I had to make everybody leave so we could..." Noah waved his hands around, not sure how to phrase it. He didn't want to be crass about his mate, but he also didn't want to sound like some romantic sap, either.

Milo clapped Noah on the back. "She's all right. We like her. I didn't think the pack would go along with a vampire as part of an alpha pair, but I've been wrong before. I also let it slip that she was the princess. I think that helped. You coming to the lake?"

"I'm going to hunt something first."

The beta nodded, then shifted and ran in the direction Sydney had blurred.

It was a testament to how strong Noah's instincts were about these wolves that he wasn't even slightly worried about Sydney being alone with them. He knew they wouldn't attack her. He also knew she could outrun them now, and given how strong she'd gotten with his blood, he had no doubt she could hold her own. Wolves were agile, but they didn't come close to the way a vampire could blur so fast they became a solid band of energy, barely detectable as a unique person-shape.

Noah breathed in the night air and closed his eyes. He focused on the night sounds, the smell of the rabbits nearby, and allowed the shift to come over him. He felt his soul pulled out of his body. It hovered there a moment, then jumped back into the wolf form.

He chased rabbits in the field, unsure if he chased them for dinner or fun. Their tiny heartbeats were so quick as they ran and hopped to escape claws and sharp teeth. Finally, he stopped toying with them and killed and ate several in succession.

When he felt satisfied, he sprinted the mile down to the lake. Sydney splashed in the water, laughing and shrieking while wolves swam near her. Even the beta had kept his wolf form, and Noah thought he knew why. In the wolf form, she wouldn't be a temptation. They wouldn't want to do things that Noah would rip them apart for. In the wolf form, only other werewolves inspired their desire. It was the same even with Noah. Although she was his mate, when he was the wolf, his mind went to a different zone. It was all hunting and playing and guarding. In those moments he was her protector and friend, not her lover.

It was sometimes hard to maintain a semblance of human-like thoughts while he was the wolf. Right now, the thing that guaranteed Sydney's safety from the other wolves was Noah's mark on her throat. It left a scent the wolves could pick up. It marked her as pack. Friend. Non-food.

He shifted to his human form and joined her in the water. She turned shy when he reached her, but he just kissed his mark on her throat.

"You okay out here?"

"I'm fine. I can't believe I'm in a lake with a pack of wolves and not getting eaten up."

Milo shifted back to his human form. "I'm going to head back and rest."

"Sure," Noah said, "You had a long day." He turned to Sydney. "Do you want to go back?"

"Gross, no. That farmhouse is terrible. I don't want to step foot inside it until I absolutely have to."

He laughed.

After a while, the pack got out of the lake and made their way back to the farmhouse. Sydney blurred past them. She was already dressed and sitting on the front porch when they got back. Little show off. Most of the wolves seemed to feel the same as she did about the farmhouse, as they spent the rest of the night under the full moon, too.

Noah laid with Sydney in the middle of a field, staring up at the stars. He tried not to let it show how much this affected him. It wasn't that he was never outside when he'd been held captive, but he'd been outside in a yard far too small for a wolf's tastes, with giant high-security fences around the perimeter. Here they had miles and miles of openness and freedom.

"I could live here," Noah said.

She punched him in the arm. "You could live anywhere. And also, oh hell no."

He laughed. "I don't mean the house. I mean the land."

"You could live at the train station. You could live here. You can probably live in Cary Town, too. You seem crazy versatile like that."

"It's true, it doesn't take much to make me happy. Just you and a place to run."

He nodded off curled beside her and didn't wake until the sun was in the sky. At first, he panicked, but then he felt their bond. Of course she hadn't combusted in the sun. The others never would have allowed it, even with Noah passed out.

He found her in the closet she'd slept in the day before. Noah shifted again and curled back up with her to wait for the sun to go down.

NOAH WOKE WHEN SYDNEY DID.

"I think the sun's up. I can kind of feel it," she said.

Noah shifted and stretched. "I'll check." He slipped out of the closet. The sun blazed in the sky.

He popped his head back in. "I can't believe you can be awake now. The sun has about an hour yet before it's safe."

She grumbled. "I want to get on the road and go home. It's so stupid that I'm waking up when I can't go anywhere."

"Once we settle some place safer, it'll be different. We'll make it sun-proof so when you wake you don't have to hide."

"Have you thought about what kind of place we might live in?" she asked, from the shadows.

"I thought I'd consult you on that. You know more about the area now than I do."

"I was thinking we could convert the Cary Town Luxury Apartments. My dad owned the penthouse. It's deserted now, but the penthouse is still set up to be vampire-friendly, and it would give us a separate space from the rest of the pack. Plus before it was apartments, it was an old hotel, so it has some similarities to what the pack is used to."

"Yeah, okay. I can deal with that. How far is it from your dad's compound?"

"About four miles, I think."

It was better than being right on top of her family. He didn't want to be negative about it, but Noah was sure the vampire king wouldn't approve of this match.

Noah returned to the cramped closet, careful not to let sunlight spill in. It was easier in his wolf form but she needed to feed. Her heart rate picked up at his proximity.

There wasn't another vampire alive that Noah would allow to feed on him. His dad would throw a fit. Noah should probably worry about the vampire king and how he'd take it, but he was more worried about his dad.

It had been a big enough issue when his mom had been brought into the pack as Cole's mate. Sure, she'd started out human, but they'd smelled vampire blood on her. It was in her veins even though she hadn't been a vampire. All they could figure was that her mother had been some vampire's thrall and he'd perhaps fed her his blood to heal her while she'd been pregnant with Jane.

Somehow that blood had made its way into the developing fetus.

The pack had accepted her, and even more so once she'd become a demon and was physically stronger, but the fact remained that wolves weren't fans of vampires, and Jane hadn't needed to drink Cole's blood.

The new pack was cool about it, but they'd just met them and hadn't been in a position to judge mate choices.

A thrill went down Noah's spine as Sydney licked the side of his neck. From another wolf it would perhaps be a sign of affection. From a human it would be a prelude to sex. From a vampire, it was like licking a piece of chocolate before you bit into it.

"Why do you think your blood makes me so strong?" Sydney asked. There was a tremor in her voice as she held back the urge to bite. She was getting so strong she was nearly his match, something he never would have thought possible when they were in the facility together and she'd been so vulnerable.

"Noah?"

"Beats me. I'm just glad it does." All those years she'd been weak and sickly, and his blood had held the cure to make her whole. If Cole wanted to make a thing of that... well Noah hadn't seen his old man in two decades. He'd gotten used to feeling orphaned. There wasn't much left to lose if his family rejected him.

Noah hissed as Sydney bit him and began to feed. His erection pressed against his pants, but they didn't have time for that. And he knew she didn't want to do it in this closet she hated. Her bite had started to create a physical response that was perhaps more disturbing than letting a vampire use him as dinner.

She ran her tongue over his throat to take the last drops of blood that trailed down. "D-did I take too much?"

"No. I'm fine," he said.

"Well, you're quiet. And you aren't..."

"It's a dirty closet, and I need to hunt. Then we need to get on the road." He shifted to face her. Even in the dark he saw her features clearly, the insecurity and fear. He planted a kiss on her cheek. "I'm just thinking. Everything is okay."

"Does this bother you? That I have to feed from you like this?"

"No. It doesn't bother me." He wasn't about to mention that it might bother his dad or the pack back home. Or how they were going to deal with the fall out from the joke fate had decided to play by putting them together. "I need to hunt."

Noah didn't want to leave her. He wanted to reassure her that they'd be fine, but he wasn't feeling it because the closer they got to getting back on the road to go home, the more his anxiety mounted. He couldn't tell Sydney because he didn't want her to worry, and he couldn't share with the pack because they needed to see him as their strong unstoppable leader. They might forgive the outburst about his imprisonment, but they wouldn't be able to deal with the instability of him showing erratic weakness every other day.

He hunted alone again and kept away from the others. He told himself it was to think, but he was brooding. He felt himself mentally going back to the cell, that space where he was alone and it was just him and his thoughts and his dreams.

Milo approached and tried to run with him, but Noah growled and snapped until he ran off. He'd be lucky if the pack was even still at the farmhouse when he returned with his behavior.

But when he got back, they were ready to go with their bikes lined up. The sun had set half an hour before, and Sydney was with them. She was the social lubricant that made this work. They felt comfortable and chatty with her. As the alpha's mate there was less pressure on her. She needed to be strong—and she was—but she didn't have to be as strong as Noah did. Or as distant.

He regretted telling them the truth about his history. Maybe he'd imagined it, but he felt sure they judged him, thought him inferior, questioned following him altogether. Maybe they followed for Sydney, and Noah was just the sideshow.

When she saw him, she excused herself and strode over. She looked like Shira. Maybe it was that she wore Shira's clothes, but she moved like her—with confidence and power. And right now Noah felt again like the visiting wolf with no home and no roots—like it was her pack, not his. Maybe it should be.

The urge came over him to shift again. He wanted to challenge her for the pack. Noah shook the thoughts from his head. He must be mad. Challenge her for the pack? What the hell? They were BOTH the alphas. Of course it was her pack. Of course she moved like an alpha. She *was* an alpha. If he couldn't keep up with that, it was his own failing. He couldn't take it out on her. He wasn't going to hurt his mate.

When she reached him, he shrugged out of her embrace and avoided her kiss. Her features betrayed hurt at his rebuff.

"Noah? Is everything okay? Are we okay?"

Why couldn't he reassure her? He'd run off earlier leaving her wondering what the hell was wrong with him, and now he was pulling away. But the thoughts he'd just had. In his head he'd shifted and ripped her apart to lead a pack of wolves he didn't even know that well. She was his fucking mate. Every part of his DNA had known she was his from the time they were babies. Even if he hadn't known what that feeling meant, even if he'd just known he was meant to protect her and be her friend. And now? What was happening to him?

What if he hurt her? What if he lost control and did something crazy because he couldn't shut this shit off?

"Noah?"

He growled. "It's fine, Sydney. Let's go. You know the way back home. We'll follow you." He smelled her tears but couldn't bring himself to comfort her.

"Did... did I do something to upset you?"

"Let's just get settled. We have bigger things to worry about right now. If the magic users go to Cary Town our families could be in danger. They may be planning something or on their way now. We don't have time."

She went back to her bike, deflated. The mood of the pack shifted in a wave as she passed them, as if they'd become emotionally entwined with her. Noah felt their resentment. Because he'd made her cry. Fuck them. It was better to make her cry than to make her bleed, and until he could trust himself not to want to hurt her for stupid things—scratch that—not to want to hurt her ever, they'd have to deal with her general unhappiness.

He ignored the accusation in their eyes and cranked his bike. Then they all followed Sydney home.

12

Sydney barely knew the way back, and yet something inside her directed her there like an internal GPS. There wasn't space in her brain to navigate; everything was Noah. It was a mistake to claim him. It was a mistake to let him mark her. So they'd been friends when they were kids. So what? He was wrong about them. If they were meant to be together, whatever was happening between them now wouldn't be happening.

Did he resent her strength? Did he find her feeding on him disgusting? Had he found his real mate in their new pack and now regretted the link with her? Maybe he was just now beginning to understand how impossible a mixed relationship could be. It wasn't just working around sleep schedules and diets. It was... everything. She belonged with another vampire. He belonged with a wolf. Nature was as it was for a reason.

Tears blurred her vision, and she was grateful for the

helmet and wind and the privacy. None of the other wolves would see or smell her tears. She needed this space to think. She blinked the tears away.

She couldn't even imagine what her father would say. She'd been so foolish thinking if she claimed Noah it would make a difference. It wouldn't make a difference. He'd kill her mate and then ground her for the next three centuries. Then she'd be back to living in a teenage holding pattern. Would her strength stay without Noah's blood or would she go back to the way she'd been before?

All she'd been to Noah was nostalgia. It was embarrassing. Of course he'd latch onto her given the circumstances he'd lived in for years. Of course he'd confuse his feelings and think she was his mate. He hadn't lived like a normal wolf. He didn't even know how to be a wolf. And now he clearly regretted everything. The wall that had gone up around him the last time she'd fed... and that distance...

Before they'd left, she'd seen something in his eyes, like he wanted to kill her. A mate's first instinct was supposed to be to protect, not whatever it was she'd seen before he'd brushed her off.

They rode straight through the night, pushing the limits of speed the bikes were capable of. Sydney was sure they could move much faster without the bikes, but they couldn't bring anything that way. Everyone had been asked to leave most of their belongings behind. It was unreasonable to ask them to give up literally everything they owned.

Even though Sydney only stopped twice to refuel, it

was a surprise when they reached Cary Town. The sun would be up soon, and although she could sense it coming, she didn't feel tired.

The Cary Town Luxury Apartments were a far cry from luxury now. The building looked condemned. Sydney pulled into the parking lot and got off the bike. The other wolves followed suit. She'd forgotten they were there for most of the trip. She'd been too busy wrapped up in her pity party, but now she was alert. She didn't sense any extra magic that would indicate the magic users from the city had beat them here, but they'd need to be on high alert until the sun went down again and they could get magic protections put on the place.

Sydney took a deep breath and took the helmet off. Any idiot would be able to tell she'd been crying. Crying made her puffy, and even vampire healing didn't seem to erase the evidence any faster than on a human. The universe seemed determined to display her misery to the world.

"It's not much, but we'll fix it up. Your dad can get us set up with electricity and water and computer tech stuff, right, Noah?"

"Yeah," he said, noncommittally.

He was almost back to the way he'd been when she'd first seen him in the cell next to hers, before she'd known he was Noah. He seemed just as dangerous and unreadable now as he had then.

"Room keys are going to be behind the front desk. They have the old-fashioned keys. They never switched to key cards before the place was deserted, so getting into rooms shouldn't be a problem. Noah and I will be in the penthouse."

The wolves followed her into the lobby. If she imagined really hard she could remember what the place had been like when she was a small child. Everything had been deep cherry paneled and gleaming and golden and sparkling with a large crystal chandelier in the center of the lobby. The walls were lined with mirrors from about halfway up the wall to the high ceilings. The floor had been such shiny tile you could see your reflection in it as you walked.

Cobwebs and dust covered everything now. Nothing was gleaming. Everything looked dull and in disrepair. Sydney caught a glimpse of herself in the clouded dirty mirror. Her demon form looked back out at her, so strong it almost overpowered the human side completely now.

Noah hadn't said a word since they left, and he still wasn't talking. Sydney ignored the tension and went to the front desk. She pulled a map from the drawer and put it on the counter. The wolves gathered around.

"Is this okay, guys? I mean, obviously it needs a lot of work, but it's got everything we need. Plenty of rooms for everyone. There's a big kitchen and a restaurant we can use for meals when we get it fixed up. There are conference rooms we can have pack meetings in. There's a gym and a pool as well as a pool on the rooftop. It's got everything. It'll just need a LOT of work to get back to how it was. And I know some magic people who might be able to help it along." It would need magic if it was ever going to go back to its former glory. Assuming Dayne and Greta and Tam and Anna agreed to help.

The pack tensed at that.

"No... they're friends," she said. But the wolves didn't seem convinced. With the exception of the witch that had given them the enchanted music, magic users were *persona non grata* with them.

Sydney took the penthouse key from the peg on the wall. "We'll have to take the stairs until the elevator is operational," she said unnecessarily. Not that any of them had trouble with stairs. Sydney could move so fast now, six flights of stairs were more like six stairs, and wolf fitness was beyond elite human athlete level. Nobody needed elevators.

The wolves studied the map and picked their own keys and Sydney headed for the stairs. She felt Noah behind her but didn't look back. She couldn't let him see her cry right now. The sun would be up soon, and she needed to get to safety.

She coughed when she pushed open the penthouse door. The dark green carpet in the hallway was thread-bare, and she squealed and jumped when a field mouse ran by. At least it wasn't a rat. Three more mice ran out behind the first one, then they squeezed under the door to the stairwell.

"Someone needs to do something about the pest problem," she said.

Noah still wasn't talking.

"I understand if, now that you're home, you think marking me was a mistake. But between that and my claim, we're tied together now. There's nothing you can do to fix it short of killing me." Maybe that was a stupid thing to say.

Noah brushed past her into the penthouse and dropped their bags on the living room sofa. Dust flew up everywhere.

"Oh dear God, what is that stench?" Sydney followed her reluctant nose into the kitchen. In the pantry, there were exploded cans of peaches everywhere. Her dad didn't eat people food. This was definitely her mom's food. "Shit, Mom, you couldn't clean out the pantry when you relocated back to the compound?" she said to the empty room.

The building was worthy of being condemned but it provided shelter, and that was all anyone needed. Nobody needed a kitchen or bathroom. The wolves could go outside. There was a freshwater spring nearby for water and bathing. And they wouldn't need heat for several months. But she wanted to live like a person, not an animal out in the woods.

She climbed the stairs to check out the rooftop. The water from the pool would have evaporated. Rainwater would collect and there would be algae likely growing on the bottom. But like everything else in this place, it could be fixed with some TLC and maybe a few incantations from Aunt Tam. Not that she'd seen Aunt Tam in years.

As she opened the rooftop door, strong arms pulled her back into the stairwell. Noah's heart pounded against her back as he nearly crushed her.

"Are you insane? Attempting suicide to get me to fucking talk to you? Jesus, Sydney."

"I-I wasn't."

Sunrise. Oh yeah. It had been a bit light when she'd opened the door. This not falling dead before sunrise thing was still hard to get used to. And she was even less tired today than she'd been recently. Even with traveling all night. She was too wired and hopped up on adrenaline and distraction. Even if she were exhausted, she had a feeling that if the sun didn't force her body to shut down, her mind wouldn't turn off and let her rest.

She'd resented the power the sun held over her all her life, the way it could command her to sleep with no argument allowed. Now she wanted it back. She'd never experienced insomnia. She didn't understand the concept. Now the idea of not being able to sleep felt terrifying.

Noah growled and dragged her down the staircase and into the main living space. She wrenched free of his grip. The red mark healed as soon as she got free.

"What the hell is wrong with you?" she asked. She rubbed her arm, even though it didn't hurt. But it had hurt a second ago, and he should know it. He shouldn't be able to get away with manhandling her like that without being subjected to some guilt.

"Me? I'm not the one who decided to experiment with vampiric sunbathing."

"I wasn't!"

"Could have fooled me. Are you blind? It's light out, and you were just going right for the door."

"What do you care? You've been weird since I got up last night. You regret it don't you? It was just being locked up so long and seeing a familiar face. I'm not really her am I?"

"Her?"

"Your true mate. It's not me."

Noah growled. "Oh for fuck's sake, of course it's you! It's always been you."

"Then why are you acting like you can't stand the sight of me? I'm sorry I'm a vampire. I can't help it, Noah. I'm sorry I need blood. I won't feed from you anymore if it disgusts you that much." She turned to flounce off into the master bedroom to deal with whatever creepy crawlies had made their home there, when two hundred pounds of angry werewolf growled and shoved her against the wall, completely ruining her flounce.

His eyes glowed golden, his fangs fighting to push through his gums. "You will feed from me. Every day. I won't let you be weak and sick again."

He pushed away from her suddenly, as if she were diseased and started to back away.

"That! Right there. What is that? If you're so insistent I feed from you, why are you doing that?"

"I can't talk about it."

Sydney's eyes glowed red. Unlike Noah she didn't fight it when her fangs burst forth. "Talk about it!" she shouted.

By now the sun was rising in the sky. It made her forehead feel prickly and odd. Her mind began to scream at her louder and louder about the sun's growing strength. But she ignored it.

The tiny windows at the top of the walls only allowed small patches of light in. They were easily avoidable. She hadn't even had a chance to see if the windows in the bedroom were still properly blacked out. And she wouldn't get a chance to because the last thing she felt was Noah's arms catching her as the sun claimed her.

When Sydney woke, she was in the master bedroom. Her dad's Botticelli hung crooked on the wall, cobwebs covering it. She couldn't believe he'd left it here. He'd always claimed it was a reproduction. But it was the original deal and priceless. Her mom had confided in her once about it. Yet he'd left it here to rot in the last fight when they'd retreated to the compound for good. He hadn't bothered to retrieve it. Maybe he'd had more on his mind than old art.

The windows were still blacked out, keeping the room dark and safe. She had no doubt the sun was still up, given the pattern of the last few days. Noah's wolf body curled around her. She could almost forget the last twenty-four hours of weirdness. Almost.

Sydney shoved her mate off her and got up. She carefully avoided the patches of light in the living room. All she wanted was to get out of here, but the sun still held her prisoner. She wanted to get the parental confrontations over with. She needed to warn them. She didn't know why the magic users hadn't come yet, but she felt certain it was only a matter of time. They knew exactly where Sydney had come from, and where she was likely going, and with the body count they'd left behind, they would surely want revenge.

Maybe they didn't care. She was an oddity, a curiosity, but both she and Noah had proven to be too much trouble, and the humans wouldn't worry the two of them might have an army to fight back.

If Noah and Sydney were more noble they'd want to

rescue all the imprisoned preternaturals, but such a thing was like saying you were going to end world hunger. It was too ubiquitous. Even if they shut down that facility, there were thousands more, located in every city that had been taken over.

The smell from the pantry was starting to get to her. The cleaning products in the hall closet had all expired. And there was no running water. She stared at the exploded peach cans. Her mother had some homemade cleaning supplies at the compound. Even if Sydney thought she could avoid her parents forever, now she had to go. She needed to get this penthouse clean. The dust and smells and cobwebs were driving her slowly insane.

She jumped when heavy hands landed on her shoulders.

"I thought perhaps you'd made another suicide attempt."

"Shut up, Noah." Was that his attempt at a joke? It wasn't even funny. It felt like they'd lost their way. As if the chemistry she'd believed they had had only been an illusion, like face-planting into asphalt after trusting the mirage of a lake.

"You need to feed."

She shrugged out of his grasp. "I don't want to feed from you. I'll hunt an animal or something."

"No! You're feeding from me. You're my mate. I have to provide for you."

The penthouse grew darker, with only moonlight coming in through the tiny thin windows now.

"Don't make it sound like such an obligation." She made a beeline for the door, but Noah was faster.

Stupid, Syd. She could have blurred up to the roof and jumped off and ran. Maybe she'd just stay gone. Let Noah run the pack himself. Inside of a week he'd be saying, "Sydney who?"

She hadn't noticed until now that he hadn't bothered to put on any clothes yet. Her eyes kept going from the muscles in his stomach to the vein in his throat. Eye candy. Dinner. Eye candy. Dinner. He could no doubt see she was losing the civilized fight as her gaze drifted back to the throbbing vein. All. That. Blood.

"I was afraid I would hurt you, okay?" Noah said. "That's why I got distant. I kept seeing how natural the pack was with you and something in me wanted to challenge you and eliminate you. I think being locked up so long really messed me up. I worry you aren't safe with me."

"You'd never hurt me."

"You don't know that. You don't know the thoughts that were going through my head. I'm scared of myself with you."

"That's bullshit."

"Sydney..."

Her eyes glowed red; her fangs elongated. If she had any doubts about him, she'd be wise not to do this before she'd fed, but whatever other insecurities she had, the idea that Noah would actually harm her wasn't one of them. They had too many other issues to deal with to be side tracked by this stupidity.

She moved into a fighting stance. "I challenge you for the pack."

Noah's eyes widened. "What? Take it back. You don't know what you just said."

"Sure I do. Which do you want more? The pack? Or me breathing? It's up to you." She punched him in the face.

His eyes glowed golden, and he began to partially shift. She knew it took everything in him not to shift completely to the wolf.

"Run, Sydney," he growled.

"No."

"I knew you were suicidal. First the sun, now this."

Sydney rolled her eyes and shoved him.

Noah growled and pounced on her, taking them both down to the ground. Looking into his eyes, she saw more wolf than man. His fangs were inches from her throat. It would be such a simple thing for him to rip it out.

"Well? One simple move, and the pack is all yours."

She closed her eyes when she felt his tongue run over the mark he'd left when he'd made her his mate.

"I told you," she whispered.

"That was so stupid. You had no way of knowing I wouldn't just kill you in a rage."

"That's not true."

Noah raised his weight off her and gave her some space. "How did you know? You thought you weren't even my true mate."

"I thought maybe you marked the wrong person, but the mark still would have protected me. When we were kids, about a year before you got taken, I was on my way to see you when I stumbled upon your parents. They were in a fight about something and it was an alpha power struggle thing, an argument they were having about the pack. She didn't use the words 'I challenge you', but she was definitely doing it. The fight turned physical, and it looked on the surface like he'd lost control. With her being a demon, she was stronger than him. But he pulled every one of his punches, anyway. He wouldn't let himself hurt her. The mate instinct is stronger than the alpha instinct."

"It could have been different with me," Noah said, still angry with her.

"No. It couldn't."

He moved closer and pulled her into his arms. "Feed, and I'll think about forgiving you for scaring the shit out of me twice today. And get out of those clothes."

The killing urge Noah had pushed away, had transformed into something else. Not that she was complaining. She'd ran off as a kid when things had turned in this direction with Noah's parents. She'd tried to bleach what she'd almost seen out of her brain with bunnies and baby deer. But as an adult in her mate's arms, she was more than happy to watch the rest of it unfold in real time.

She wriggled out of her jeans and top. As soon as she bit him, he was inside her. They were both still. He didn't thrust, and she didn't drink. They just stayed that way. She couldn't read his mind, but somehow she knew he felt what she felt. A completeness, as if the last day had been erased entirely. He began to move slowly within her as she drank, and everything felt right again.

13

Noah sat beside a stream with Sydney while she finished bathing, alert for anyone who shouldn't be out here. He was both irritated and embarrassed with how she'd played him earlier, but if she hadn't done it, things would have grown colder and colder between them. As long as he could trust that the mating instincts were stronger than the other wolf instincts, he knew he could protect her.

He'd been sure that being kept prisoner had turned him wrong somehow, but it was garden variety wolf nature—something he would have known if he'd been raised normally. If anything, the facility had forced him to suppress all the things that were natural, causing them to grow even larger in his mind.

Sydney put her jeans and T-shirt on. "We have to go talk to our parents. We should split up."

Noah growled. "We aren't splitting up. We'll go together."

"Noah, I need to talk to my family alone. And so do you. You know how they'll be if we go together. And we don't have time. We have to warn them so they can strengthen the wards. And we need our place warded as well."

He sighed. "I know. Just be careful... If anything happened to you..."

"I know. I'm fast now. I'll be okay."

Noah watched her blur through the trees. When she was gone, he began to pick his way through the forest, his senses on high alert. If he could remember Sydney's scent after all this time, surely he could also remember family.

After a few miles, he caught a scent he recognized and followed it through the forest until he saw the outline of the entrance to the hive. The hive was what the pack called their den because the interlocking network of underground caves resembled a beehive. It had always been heavily warded both with magic and tech. Noah had no doubt, given his dad's nearly supernatural computing skills, that the cave's technological security was as strong as ever.

He took a deep breath and began to pace. In theory, he'd wanted nothing more than to be reunited with his family and to be free. But now, with the prospect of them mere yards away...

Noah had to fight the urge to flee. It would be so much easier to run, but his mother had a direct connection to the demon world. They needed Tam and the demons. They needed to rebuild Cary Town.

He pushed past the large branches that grew over the

mouth of the cave and stepped inside. It was dark well into the cave. He bumped into solid steel. A computer touch pad lit up at his nearness and a robotic female voice said: "Please state your business." A second steel wall came down behind him, blocking his exit.

"Please state your business," the voice said again.

Noah tried to speak, but the voice was too similar to the one he'd heard every day for years of his captivity, and the steel walls trapping him didn't help. The logic that family and safety was behind this door couldn't penetrate the flashback.

He'd had to be so strong. For the pack. For Sydney. Now that he had privacy, it all started to unravel. He felt himself like a tightly wound ball of twine, slowly coming undone.

"State your business!"

Noah backed up until he hit the other wall. The fear overwhelmed him, and he shifted and huddled his wolf body as far from the screaming computer as he could get.

The door slid open to reveal several members of the pack, armed. Noah howled, a long mournful howl, and a second later a black metal rectangle was jabbed into his side, and everything went dark.

When he woke, he was in a glass-enclosed room that was far too familiar for comfort, lying on a table, wrapped in a sheet. Then he smelled the salt and heard the quiet crying of his mother.

"Mom?"

Jane was as beautiful as ever. But then, not ever aging would do that for you.

"I can't believe you're alive. I hoped, but I didn't think I'd ever see you again."

He took another look around the room. It was the pack's clinic—a glassed room at the back of the hive where pack members who needed medical care went. Werewolves healed so fast that it was rarely used, but if silver was involved in an attack, or if a wolf got sick, it came in handy. It was good to keep a sick wolf quarantined from the others. They rarely got sick, but when they did, it was impressively bad and dangerous.

"Where's dad?"

"He's hunting. Blake went out to find him. Sorry about the tazer. The guards grew up with you but they didn't remember your scent. When you blacked out, you shifted back, and one of them thought you looked like Cole and brought you in. What happened? Tam and Dayne did spells for years, but we couldn't find you."

"I was in a city. They kept me in a glass cell and..."

Jane glanced around the room. "Oh. I'm so sorry. You know your dad and his tech aesthetic." She looked down at her hands. "And the security at the front... we didn't know. Cole... he's gotten more paranoid since you were taken. I thought the security was ridiculous before, but now... It's just a whole other level."

Noah reached out and took her hand. "Mom. You're rambling. I'm okay." It was strange being here again. He'd been in captivity longer than he'd ever lived with his parents. Jane felt alien to him, but he would never say it. She was in too much pain, and he wouldn't be able to properly explain what he meant without hurting her more.

She broke down into sobs. He'd been trying to make things lighter, not worse.

"It's just... I lost you when you were a baby, and then we got you back and only had you for a few years before... And now... you're all grown and I missed all that time. I missed all those years of your childhood. I missed your teens. I'm afraid if I close my eyes or look away you'll be gone again, and I'll miss something else."

There was a growl from the doorway. Noah looked up to see his dad glaring at his throat.

"Who the fuck bit and claimed you?!"

Oh right. That.

"Cole!" Jane said. "He's been held prisoner for years. It's not his fault!" So his mom had noticed the claim, too. She'd just had the good sense to keep her mouth shut about it.

"I will kill the vampire that marked my child," Cole said.

Noah growled. "You will not touch a hair on my mate's head."

A sick look came over the alpha. "You *allowed* a vampire to mark you? It wasn't just some fucked-up experiment?"

"Well, *allowed* is a strong word," Noah said. "I knew she was my true mate, but she marked me first before I could stop her. She wanted our lifespans to match." When he said it out loud to explain it, it was sort of sweet and logical.

The alpha growled again, pacing the metallic floor. "There is no way that a *vampire* is your true mate. If you expect me to believe... Whatever happened to you when you were locked up must have messed with your mind. She must have done something to make you believe..."

A throat cleared. Jane had gotten control of her tears. "Umm, hi, Cole. Remember your mate, Jane? The one who started out human and was only mystically able to be your true mate because of the vampire blood that somehow was part of my genetic makeup? It's a fun story. I could break out the slides."

"That's different. It's different. You and I are... You weren't a vampire!"

"It's not from being locked up," Noah said. "It's Sydney."

"Ha!" Jane said. "I told you. I told you when they were toddlers. I called it. You should have just let him feed her when they were small. There was no stopping this."

Cole rounded on Noah again. "Are you feeding her? She's weak and sick and... a vampire. And if you're feeding her..."

"If I'm feeding her then what, Dad? I thought you'd be glad to see me. I thought you'd miss your fucking son and be glad I was all right. It's been two decades. I wasn't expecting balloons and streamers, but I thought you'd at least give a shit."

The alpha spun on his heel and stormed out of the sick bay.

Jane's eyes glowed red, and she partially shifted into the demon form: red scaled skin and black claws. Noah reached out and took her hand, and she melted back into her normal human visage.

"It's okay," he said.

"It really isn't. But he'll come around. You just have to

give him time. He doesn't deal well with reunions. He doesn't know how to process it, so he lashes out at the first thing that doesn't line up with what he's used to."

Under most circumstances, Cole was solid and dependable. But certain scenarios set off his less-than-reasonable side. This appeared to be one of them. If stories were true, his mom's transition to demon had been another.

"I need you to get him to come to the Cary Town Luxury Apartments, to the roof," Noah glanced at the wall clock, "in two hours. We're going to have a meeting. Get Uncle Cain and Aunt Tam. And Uncle Dayne and Aunt Greta. We could all be in danger. Dad needs to put this stuff aside for a night or two, then he can hate me all he wants to."

Jane brushed the hair out of his face. "Oh, honey, he doesn't hate you. He's just how he is. You'll understand if you ever have your own pack."

Noah cleared his throat. "I... um... sort of have my own pack. We're staying at the apartments. When Dad gets over his snit, I need his help with electrical wiring and security if he's not disowning me."

"I'll talk to him."

Jane left Noah alone, and he scrambled back into his clothes, hoping his mate was having better luck.

14

Sydney had lurked outside the compound for over an hour. She couldn't just walk in there. At some point someone had to come outside. As if the universe heard her thought, a side metal door swung open, and one of her dad's guards stepped out. He carried a large human military-grade weapon. Despite vampire speed and fangs, sometimes a gun was still more menacing. It depended on what species the threat was.

Their primary enemy was human, and sometimes a bullet got to a magic user better. Fangs were too close, and if they'd ingested something as a vampire deterrent it was best not to have any of their blood. It was too easy for them to turn the tables on a cocky fang-happy vampire.

Sydney had changed at the last minute into a turtleneck, hoping her father wouldn't question the clothing choice. Vampires didn't always dress seasonally, anyway. She tugged at the fabric to cover Noah's mark. Maybe her dad wouldn't smell it before she had a chance to figure out how to tell him.

She jumped out of the tree she'd been sitting in, and the gun swung toward her. She threw her arms up. "Reynard, it's just me."

The vampire's eyes glowed a dangerous red, and his fangs dropped. "Where the fuck have you been, Syd? The king is going to kill you. He almost killed me for letting you out of my sight. Then where would my mate have been? You think Anthony would let Persephone hang around the compound without a vampire protecting her? He'd toss her out on her ass. How would she survive all by herself out here? You don't think about anything but yourself and your own petty dramas. Did the little princess get tired of being locked in the tower?"

Sydney shrugged, feeling once again like she'd regressed in age back to the teen years. They'd always treated her like a kid. They'd never once seen her as an adult. She wanted to shove her dad's vampire goon back on his ass. He deserved it. The shock and surprise on his face would be worth it. But she wasn't ready to play that card yet. Let them think she was the same weakling that had run away.

He cocked his head to the side. "Get in there. Don't make me drag you in kicking and screaming. If I accidentally shoot you, you might bleed out before we can find you someone to eat."

"Maybe my dad will kill you, then I can have your mate."

Reynard growled. "If you weren't the princess..."

"You'd what?"

"You have no idea little girl. And you don't want to."

The urge was strong to wipe the smug smile off his face. He thought her only safety and protection was who she was. He had no idea how much the game had changed.

None of them would let her feed off their mates. Jacob had been her only human food source for years. Anthony could have made them all share, but Sydney suspected he had enough trouble dealing with the possibility of what she'd done with Jacob while feeding. The visual of girl-on-girl action would be way too much for him to cope with.

Sydney pulled the door open and turned back. "What kind of mood is he in?"

"Just go. He's only had one mood since you left. Bad."

She took a deep breath and went up the stairs. It was quieter than she remembered. The main living area was empty. Ordinarily around this time it was loud with everyone chattering away. It was as if the entire compound had fallen asleep or died when she'd left.

Sydney wandered the halls until she found her father's study. The door was cracked just enough to let light out. She knocked.

"Leave me in peace," he growled.

"Dad?"

Anthony blurred to the door and jerked it off its hinges. His eyes glowed red. He was livid, but he crushed her in a hug, anyway. He quickly got control of himself and backed off. "I'm sorry, did I hurt you?"

"A little," Sydney lied. Something told her not to show her hand too soon.

He shoved her sleeves up to inspect her arms for bruises while she hoped he couldn't tell what was different about her.

"Where were you?" he demanded. "I sent out search parties. One of them is still out looking for you. Your mother and I have been worried sick. She'll hardly eat. I've been giving her my blood to keep her strong."

Lie your ass off!

Her dad looked gaunt. She hadn't been gone long, but in that time the vampire had defied the laws of vampirism and seemed to have aged decades.

Typically, she was a terrible liar, but with any luck he'd be so happy to have her home, he'd believe anything she could string together into a coherent sentence. And weren't the best lies peppered with truth?

"Jacob kidnapped me. He made me write the letter. He had some deal to be reunited with his family by some magic users."

"I'll torture him slowly. Then I'll kill him."

"He's already dead."

"How did you get away?"

"I didn't." And this was where she had to tread carefully. Noah's dad had probably been much cooler about all this. "Do you remember Noah?"

"The wolf?" Anthony asked.

Sydney nodded, hoping her face didn't give anything more away. She hoped she didn't look smitten.

"How could I forget him. That stupid pup wouldn't leave your side when you were little." The bitterness edged into his voice. "I'd thought that perhaps if you could feed from him you'd get stronger, but Cole wouldn't have it. Selfish asshole."

She was tempted to confess the full story now. If it had been her dad's idea to let her drink from Noah, surely he couldn't be too upset if she was mated to him, but a cowardly voice inside her head warned her not to tell.

"He was being kept in the same facility they kept me in. He recognized me and broke out and broke me out with him."

Anthony's eyes narrowed as if he could see the whirlwind romance unfolding before him. "And where is your wolf hero now?" His eyes flashed, but he quickly covered it.

It was too late. Sydney had seen it. If Noah had done anything more than just bust her out and bring her home, her father would kill him.

"He's at your old penthouse."

A territorial growl.

Sydney pressed on. "We're afraid the magic users might come here. Cary Town looks abandoned, so maybe they did a quick sweep and assumed everybody moved on, or maybe they're making plans and will show up when we least expect it. We're having a meeting tonight on the rooftop. The wards need to be stronger. We need to rebuild the city."

"What is all this 'we'? What are you going to do, Syd? I love you, but you know your involvement will be minimal. I think it's for the best if you stay here at the compound. I'll go to the meeting. You need to stay where you'll be safe and conserve your strength."

"No way. I'm going."

"And why would you want to do that? Sydney, if there is something you're not telling me... If that filthy wolf touched you, I will kill him."

"N-no, he didn't. N-nothing like that." *Lie your ass off!* "I just want to go."

"You will stay here. Your mother has been beside herself."

"W-where is she?"

"She's in our room."

Her parents' room was underground at the end of the hallway opposite from the stairs.

"Charlotte, you have a visitor," Anthony said, pushing Sydney into the room.

Her mother bolted up in bed. "Syd? Is that you?"

"It's me." Despite the lie she'd told her father, the guilt over the truth ate at her now that she was dealing with her mom. She'd wanted freedom, but not at this expense.

"When you're father claimed me, he said I'd never get sick. The big fat liar."

Mystical bonds didn't seem to cover the pain of losing someone you loved.

The door slammed behind her, the lock turned into place. Sydney banged against the steel. "Dad, open this door!"

"Never! You are never leaving this compound again!"

"But Jacob..." If he believed her story, how could he see any of this as her fault?

"I don't care. I don't want you near that wolf. If he

risked life and limb to bring you back here there can be only one thing he wants."

"Oh. My. God. Dad, I'm twenty-seven. Who the hell cares if that's what he wants? Do we have to have the nun conversation again?"

"Syd, I'm not in the mood for this right now," her dad growled from the other side of the door. "Reynard is out here. We'll figure out something for you to eat when I return from this meeting."

"Dad! You're being insane!" But there was no response. He was already on his way to the penthouse.

"This is bullshit!" Sydney shouted. "I am fucking going to that meeting!"

Her mother winced. "You know how your father gets. You're stuck here until he decides to open that door. With me in here, it'll be sooner rather than later. Be glad for that, at least."

Sydney sighed. "I hate to leave with you like this, but I'm going. I need to be there with Noah."

Charlee's eyes were shrewd. "There's something going on with that wolf isn't there?"

Sydney buckled and told her mother about the mating link. She felt guilty, as if she'd run off to elope.

"So, I have to be there. I can't leave my mate and pack alone to deal with everyone—not with Noah just now being free after so long. He tries to hide it, but even under the best circumstances he gets overwhelmed around too many people. And tensions could be high."

"They always are when everyone gets together. But that's reinforced steel, you'll never—"

Sydney wasn't sure if her mother had finished that

sentence because she'd already blurred to the door and pounded through it. Her dad's guard was waiting for her on the other side. He startled, fumbling with his gun at human-speed. Sydney ripped the weapon from his hand, emptied the chamber and took the magazine. She'd at least learned something useful in her time at the compound. She pushed him with all her strength.

He went flying through the air until his back hit the wall at the end of the hallway and he slumped down, eyes wide.

"Don't get up," she said. "You can't take me."

"Sydney?"

She turned back to her mother. "I'd love to explain this, but I have a meeting to get to."

"At least I know you can take care of yourself. Be careful, and try not to rile your father up too much. You know how he gets."

"Thanks, Mom."

"Watch out!" Charlee said.

Reynard had gotten behind her and was trying to put her in a choke hold. Sydney flipped him hard on the concrete so hard his back cracked. Even with his mate's blood, he was looking at a good half hour healing time for that. "I *said*, stay down," Sydney said. How he'd managed to stay in her father's employ with his sub par listening skills was anybody's guess.

Sydney blurred out of the building and didn't slow until she reached the Cary Town Luxury Apartments. A few of the more intimidating male pack members stood outside the front door. They nodded as she approached.

"If a vampire shows up with dark hair and thick

eyebrows... looks sort of like a caveman, acts sort of like a caveman... don't let him in. He's not on the guest list."

"Yes Ma'am," one of them said and saluted.

"Don't salute. This isn't a military installation."

He shrugged, and she went inside. It was still hard to get used to the way the place had fallen into disrepair, but the wolves had already been hard at work on it. She had no idea what they'd used for cleaning products. She'd heard a few of the girls were quite crafty, maybe they'd made something, but it was obvious they'd been hard at work on the lobby.

The cobwebs had been cleared away and the mirrors gleamed as much as they could at this stage. Everything was clean, but it was still dark as a tomb without electricity. One of the wolves had helpfully put an "out of order" sign on the elevator, as if anyone would try to utilize it.

She took the stairs two at a time to the sixth floor where a few more pack members were stationed. They nodded, but happily no one saluted this time.

She was surprised they'd cleaned the hallway and the penthouse. The rotted peach smell was gone. She could get used to being part of an alpha pair. Still more pack wolves stood outside the stairs leading to the roof.

"Let me guess, we have more goons at the top?"

Milo smirked. "Nothing gets by you."

"Nice job on the clean-up by the way," she said.

"No problem. We still have a lot of work, but we at least wanted to get the areas guests would see."

"Is everybody here?"

"I think so. Noah gave me a list, but there were a couple of unexpecteds."

Sydney raised a brow. "Oh?" They must have been okay if they'd been waved up.

"Yeah, but we knew them."

"How did *you* know them?"

"Small world, I guess, but it was that witch that gave us our music and her panther."

Weird.

Sydney took the last flight of stairs two at a time. She was halfway up them when she heard the vampire king roar "What the fuck do you mean she's your mate!?!"

Maybe she should slink away, but her conscience got the better of her. She couldn't leave Noah alone with her dad, especially since her mate's new immortality was just as conditional as hers.

The metal door clanged against the brick wall, announcing her arrival.

"Sydney? You didn't tell him?"

The wounded look on Noah's face nearly killed her. As if she'd betrayed him or as if he didn't matter to her now that they were all back home.

"Well... I mean... He already locked me in the compound with a vampire guard when I *didn't* tell him. What do you think he would have done with more information?"

Noah growled, the fur starting to crop up on his arms. Sydney rushed to stand between her father and her mate. "We have more important stuff to deal with."

The vampire king suddenly looked more pained than angry. "I'm so disappointed in you Syd. I can't believe you'd let a wolf..."

She knew it was wrong, but she shoved her father

like she'd shoved his guard. He flew across the rooftop until he landed against the brick wall. Everyone went quiet.

The king looked up, and for a second she thought she'd only made things worse.

"You're strong," he said.

"Yeah."

Anthony got up and blurred to her, crushing her in a hug. "You're strong!"

Was he actually crying?

"Okay, dad. It's getting a little weird."

Anthony backed off and wiped his face with the back of his hand. She'd never seen a display of emotion like this from him, and suddenly it became clear what her mother saw in him. Despite all their romantic behavior, it had always seemed like an act with her father. And now she realized why. She'd never seen him show a strong emotion except for anger. This was the first time she'd seen him cry.

There was another moment of frozen silence, as if everyone assembled had been put on pause. But then Anthony cleared his throat and took a seat at the table.

That was it? She'd expected that he would never accept Noah as her mate. She'd expected him to try to drive them apart or keep her under lock and key, that it might even come to bloodshed, that she might have to go far away and never speak to him again.

"Well?" he said pointedly at Noah, "Don't we have important things to discuss?"

Noah was as weirded out as Sydney, but in an odd

way it felt as if the vampire king had actually just given his blessing. Or as close to it as they were going to get.

Cole, was another matter. Now that the vampire king's threat had been neutralized, it only drew more attention to the werewolf alpha who still seemed unhappy with the situation. He growled quietly from his seat, his eyes golden and deadly.

"Look on the bright side," Anthony said, "We're permanent allies now."

Did her dad just smile? Like *smile*? It might be time to look for alien pods.

Cole growled in response.

Sydney turned to Noah. She knew he must see the questions and hurt in her eyes. Did the werewolf alpha not like her? She'd been so worried about her dad's reaction, the thought that the wolves wouldn't want her around, stung. Especially in light of the pack she was already half running with Noah. It wasn't like she couldn't fit in with wolves. She'd already proven that she could.

"He'll get over it," Noah whispered, pressing a kiss to her forehead.

Jane got up from her seat next to Cole and wrapped Sydney in a hug. "Welcome to the family, dear," she said.

The alpha werewolf growled again.

"That's it," Jane said. "What's done is done. You're hurting Sydney."

"You know I have nothing against her, personally. It's the *vampire thing,*" he spat, his arms crossed over his chest now like a petulant toddler demanding a cookie.

Right, because hating Sydney's race had nothing to do with her or anything.

Anthony had shifted from psychopathic rage, to acceptance, to near beaming and giddy in the space of about five minutes. "We should have a party for them," he said.

Everyone just stared.

"What? We've been hiding out and barely talking for years, let's throw a party for once, to celebrate the joining of our two mini-kingdoms, so to speak."

And now he was back to strategizing, calculating, and controlling. The vampire king simply couldn't help himself, but at least he didn't seem to have goals of world domination in mind this time.

When Sydney had been told the stories, her mother kept saying that it was because he wanted to protect them. Charlee's explanation was starting to sound true, rather than the lies a woman told herself to excuse her husband's crimes. Not that her parents had ever married in the human way.

A throat cleared at the end of the table. Uncle Cain. He stood. "Why don't we secure our borders, and then we can talk about parties?"

Anthony growled, and Noah didn't look thrilled. It didn't matter who got together, Cain always ran things one way or another. Maybe he simply had more focus than the rest of them.

Aunt Greta slid into the seat next to Sydney and gave her a hug. "I've missed you," She said. "I wish the circumstances of this reunion were different."

Sydney couldn't imagine a happy set of circumstances in which they'd all hang out together again. For years they'd lived a few miles from one another but mostly avoided each other, various feuds and spats getting in the way.

"Hey kid," Dayne said. The sorcerer smiled and joined Greta.

"Hey Uncle Dayne."

She'd spent many weekends as a child in his cottage basement watching him concoct potions and testing some of them for him. Though her dad didn't know about that part. Anthony might have murdered the sorcerer if he'd known she'd been helping him perfect potions that turned people into stink bugs.

On the other side of the table was Hadrian, a vampire who used to work for her father. She'd only heard of him. She'd never met him. He'd been a priest once and now lived in the basement of the local abandoned church. There was a rumor that he could go out in the sun for short periods without burning, but it was probably just a rumor.

Sydney knew it was him because she'd met his mate, Angeline, a few times over the years. Hadrian and her father hadn't spoken since Sydney was a baby from what she'd heard. He'd betrayed them all and helped line up the events that had brought on the war. So this fantastic existence she'd had? Probably Hadrian's fault.

He squirmed in his seat, clearly uncomfortable facing everyone again. But Angeline was a guardian, and as a fallen angel she was strong and could help in the fight. They both were. It was the least he owed them.

"Hey, missed you."

Sydney looked up, startled. Anna stood in the middle of the table. Not *on* the table, in the middle of it. She was Luc's mate and also a witch. But her ability to permeate solid objects like a ghost came from her demon mate—Uncle Cain's brother.

"Anna, will you please stop doing that?" Luc said.

"No, Sweetie, but thank you for asking. I'm about over this not being able to hold a solid form unless you're touching me, thing. It's been like thirty years of this!"

"I told you it would last a century or so. Then once all your other demon powers have developed, you'll be able to go solid on your own. It's for your protection."

"No, you said a couple of decades, not a century!"

"Did I? I forget," Luc said. "Time runs together for me. Maybe I meant a few decades."

"Luc! It better not be a century!"

Anna had always been difficult. Sydney hadn't seen her in over ten years, but she remembered that much. Nobody complained about banal shit quite like Anna did.

"Oh just grab her," Cain said, annoyed.

"I can't without her getting stuck in the table," Luc said.

"Yes, it would hurt. And then she wouldn't do it anymore."

Anna rolled her eyes and got out of the table. Luc held her hand so she could sit down.

Only one person at the meeting hadn't spoken to anyone, a guy in a black leather jacket. He sat next to a strange blonde woman who'd been making small talk with a squirrel. They were the two that weren't on the guest list. He looked like a hit man, and Sydney wasn't entirely sure he wasn't there to eliminate them.

"Okay, that's enough!" Cain said, growing tired of the meet and greet and wacky antics.

When everyone settled, the demon leader continued. "When Jane came to us a few hours ago about the meeting, we weren't as surprised as you might expect. Tam, why don't you take this? You explain the magic stuff better."

Tam stood as Cain sat down. "Some of you may know that I had a very dear friend decades ago who was my familiar for a long time. He was a raven therian and traveled with me extensively. Henry is in the angelic realm now. Though we closed the portals to physically come here, communication is still possible in dreams and vision states. I asked Henry to do reconnaissance and bring some information back to me."

Sydney found her hand in the air like an overeager school child.

"Yes?" Tam said.

"How do you know it wasn't just you imagining him? How do you know it was really your friend?" Tam had a reputation for magic, but dreams and visions felt too unreal to bet your life on.

"I didn't do this today. Henry came to me two days ago. He told me you guys were on your way but that the magic users in the hub city wouldn't be far behind." She looked apologetic. "I didn't say anything because if you didn't make it back, I didn't want your parents to mourn you twice. And there was always a chance my information could be wrong."

Jane and Cole nodded their understanding, but Anthony looked like he wanted to kill her for withholding information.

Tam ignored him and continued. "The people in the city waited because they didn't want to just chase you down and kill you. They want to eradicate what is left of our city and take everyone who survives the fight back with them. It's a capture, not a kill mission. Those require more planning."

It hadn't occurred to Sydney that they wouldn't simply rush up there seeking quick vengeance. The risk of death, she'd weighed and accepted. She hadn't considered the horror of recapture or the capture of her family and friends as well.

"Are you okay, Syd?" Tam asked.

"I-I'm fine," she lied.

Tam arched a brow but went back into her speech. "Even from the beyond, Henry has watched out for me. When I told Cain about it, he suggested the same as you, that maybe it was just a dream. But I started preparing, anyway. When Jane told us of the meeting tonight, I got to say 'I told you so.'"

Cain chuckled from beside her.

"Jane and Cole know Fiona," Tam said. The blonde stranger gave a shy wave from beside the panther therian in the leather jacket whose arm she clutched as if he might keep her from going beneath the surface of the sea and drowning. "Fiona and Z took Noah in when he was just a pup after Jane died that one time."

Z. Yeah, he looked like a one-letter-for-a-name sort of guy.

Jane stifled a laugh.

"What's funny?"

"After Jane died that one time," Jane said. "I love how casual you are about my untimely demise."

"Eh, you came back," Tam said. Mystical deaths and resurrections and changing species was just another day for the bad ass superwitch turned demon mate. "Anyway," she said, preparing to go back into catching the group up.

"Ummm, can I?" Fiona asked from the table. "It's my story."

"Sure, why not," Tam said.

"Some of you met me that time we had that big fight with Anthony." She pushed a long strand of blonde hair behind her ear.

Big fights with Anthony were fairly commonplace, but the group seemed to know which specific big fight she was talking about. Anthony had the good grace to look ashamed. He had briefly kidnapped Fiona, after all.

Sydney had still been in the womb when all this had gone down, but she'd heard the stories about fifty times, mostly from Noah when they were kids, who she was sure had exaggerated what he'd heard from his parents. The story had directly involved Noah, as he'd been the one Anthony had taken to try to get Cole to spill the beans about his den's secret location.

Fiona continued. "I wasn't a very good witch back then. I was too scared of my powers and of everything else. It didn't become an issue until I spotted my first gray hair. Because I wasn't using magic to the extent and level that other magic users were, I was aging like a regular human. Meanwhile I knew Z could live centuries. I panicked and looked Tam up. She taught me how to grow and channel my power. So that's why I'm here, to help. I-I can talk to the animals."

Talking to the squirrel made sense now.

"It's a rare gift," Tam said. "And it's one we're going to use to our advantage. The forests around here are teeming with deer, coyotes, wolves, bears, and birds. Without the humans around encroaching on their habitats, the wild areas have gotten very wild. We can use magic, but with only magic, we're simply fighting them with what they already know to expect. When the wildlife comes after them as well, it might change their vindictive outlook. Once we fight them back, we can strengthen and create strong magical wards to keep them out in the future. But we don't have time for that now. We didn't have time for it two days ago. We'll need the right moon and a lot of magic users. It's not something we can do under pressure or deadline. But we can fight. We're good at fighting."

Anthony interrupted Tam. "I let us down."

The group seemed startled by the admission. Her father admitting to doing anything wrong was pretty much unheard of.

"It was foolish to try to control everything and everyone like I did. It was for Sydney and Charlee, but it got out of hand. If I hadn't set up a police state—no matter the overall good I intended for my family—it couldn't have been taken over in so many places by the humans. We wouldn't have had to hide and stay invisible like this.

I ushered us into another dark ages for our kind. I'm sorry."

Everyone at the table sort of sat in a freeze frame until Cain clapped the vampire king on the back. "It takes a big person to admit to that."

Anthony seemed to search for a joke or insult, but it wasn't there to find.

Tam closed her eyes, and the wind swept up around her as she lapsed into a trance. When she opened her eyes again, she looked panicked.

"They're coming. They'll be here in less than an hour. They're moving fast."

"I'll start my part," Fiona said.

Tam nodded. "I'll get everyone else ready."

"I'll go with her," Sydney blurted out.

"No," Noah said, "I don't want us to get separated."

Sydney felt her eyes flash, and her fangs begin to push out. Noah must have seen her resolve and realized that now wasn't the time for a challenge fight between an alpha pair. He nodded slowly as if to convince those assembled that it was his call, and he'd decided to be magnanimous with his mate.

Sydney didn't need permission. She was finished getting permission to go on walks. She wouldn't be locked inside compounds or cells or penthouses or dens any longer. She'd lost all her taste for cages.

15

Sydney followed Fiona through the woods. She was surprised the witch's panther mate had stayed behind with the others, but Z seemed like a fighter by nature. He'd want to hear the plan for the big confrontation.

Fiona pushed a long strand of blonde hair out of her face with one hand and pulled back a tree branch with the other. Sydney grabbed the branch before it could thwap her in the face. While nice, Fiona seemed off in her own world and perhaps a little scatterbrained.

Sydney hadn't felt any particularly strong connection to the witch, she just wanted to get away from the discomfort of not being accepted by Noah's dad.

Every few minutes, Fiona made various animal calls, but it was clear she wasn't mindlessly calling like a hunter in the forest seeking to mimic. She knew and spoke their language. A line of animals formed behind them and followed as she collected more for her menagerie.

Many were natural enemies and shouldn't be able to be together without fighting. Sydney wasn't sure what the witch had told them to make them play nice, but whatever it was, they'd jumped the moment she called.

As they moved through the woods, a green glowing mist trailed off the witch. She seemed like a siren to the woodland creatures as the group grew ever larger.

"So," Fiona said when they reached a clearing, "You don't know me. Why did you want to join me for the boring work?"

Watching the witch expertly communicate with the animals and get such varying species to come along for their plan was anything but boring.

"It was too much back there with everyone. I was about to come out of my skin." If she'd been more thoughtful, she would have suggested Noah go on this mission, instead. If anyone needed space and to get away from everyone, it was her mate. But Sydney knew he would have refused, insisting on acting as a pack leader. In just a few days he'd become attached to his new role. It was good for him to get out of his shell. He still needed to prove himself, and wandering off in the woods at a time like this wouldn't accomplish that goal.

"I know what you mean," Fiona said. She paused when a crow swooped down and started squawking at her. She squawked back. The bird became enraged and dove toward her. She lifted a hand, flicked her wrist, and the bird went sailing back several yards. "Crows are seriously such pessimists." She squawked once more and the bird flew away.

"You don't like crowds, either?" Sydney asked.

"I used to be a shut in. Agoraphobia. I was a prisoner in my own home for years because the birds kept telling me that if I left my house something bad would happen."

Sydney could relate in a way. It wasn't fear that had held her captive in her own home, but she'd been a prisoner since childhood all the same. "How'd you get over it?"

"Z kidnapped me because he needed a babysitter for Noah. I'm glad Noah's okay, by the way. I was sad to hear when he'd been taken. I know how heartbroken Jane and Cole were when they lost him the first time." Fiona stopped walking, and the animals stopped as well. She turned to Sydney. "Cole will accept you eventually. Just give it some time."

Sydney nodded, concerned that perhaps Fiona could read her mind or something.

"Wait, Z kidnapped you?"

"Yeah, but I don't think it's because he wanted a babysitter."

Given the couple's relationship now, Sydney was pretty sure about that as well.

Fiona continued through the meadow, speaking to each animal in turn. Some—like rabbits—she dismissed or maybe told to hide. Sydney thought hundreds of aggressive hoppy rabbits might be just as intimidating as all the rest of the assembled wildlife.

"Why are we bringing deer?" she asked. When one

thought of hardcore animal fighters, one did not usually picture deer.

"They're normally quite docile, except during mating season. But they can kick like hell. I wasn't sure they'd come, but they agreed. Who am I to turn away good help?"

An explosion sounded in the distance. Sydney turned to see sparks of red and purple and green and blue rising into the air. The magic users were there; the fight had already started. It was much faster than she'd anticipated, even with Tam's warning that they were on their way. What if Noah and Sydney had gotten home just a few hours later than they had? They would have walked in on the fighting. At least Tam had a few days warning.

Fiona moved faster, speaking each species' language as she reached new animals. Each time, the animals gathered others of their kind and joined them.

When Sydney and Fiona made it down the hill, the melee had begun in earnest. It was almost impossible to tell who was on which side as sparks and incantations flew. Fiona raised her arms as glowing green light trailed from her hands, wavy like strands of electric hair.

Hundreds of animals both predator and prey, running and flying, had paused, waiting for her command. Fiona dropped her hands, and the animals flew into the fray, attacking and distracting the magic users who had come to do them harm.

"Leave no one alive," Tam shouted from a few hundred yards away. "I've already got a messenger." She held a young scrawny man with red hair by the scruff of the neck. Then she trapped him in a band of energy.

Sydney flinched at the order to kill everyone, even though she knew the score here. It was kill or be killed. Leaving survivors would just create a larger, angrier army to deal with later. Decimating their numbers was the only hope they might be left in peace.

Tam and Cain had brought in hundreds of demons from the demon dimension. They'd no doubt used a nearby portal while Fiona and Sydney had been out collecting animals. Even before the animals were introduced into the fray, the magic users were beginning to become overwhelmed by the demons they hadn't expected to fight.

Maybe Uncle Cain felt guilty for staying out of the war years earlier. It hadn't been his fight, and he'd refused to send his kind in to help. The preternaturals might have lost anyway, even with the demons. It was a big war. This, by contrast, was a battle, and the troops the magic users had sent in were ill-prepared to cope with hoards of unexpected demons and all the local wildlife turning on them, too.

Cain and Luc fought with the rest of them, creating a buffer for Tam, Anna, and Dayne to do defensive magic. Aunt Greta was nowhere to be found, but she wouldn't be. Except for being able to shapeshift into a housecat, she didn't have any real powers to speak of. She had more than human strength but she wasn't strong enough for a fight like this. And she couldn't do magic.

Sydney heard a hiss and looked up. A black cat sat on a limb high in the tree above her. The cat's body was arched in angry panic. So maybe Aunt Greta hadn't gone home. She'd pushed through her fear to stay near Dayne.

Fiona wandered up. The witch was wiped out from the magic and commanding the animals. Aunt Greta meowed at her, and Fiona communicated back.

"Dayne will be okay. I'll head that way."

The black cat looked mollified but climbed higher in the tree and kept her worried gaze in Dayne's direction.

Noah fought nearby with a magic user Sydney recognized. It was the woman he'd let go on the night of their escape. What was her name again? Sydney edged closer.

"Kristen, I spared you once," Noah said. "I can't do it again."

But Sydney saw the pain on her mate's face, and knew that if he could, he'd spare her a second time. Irrational jealousy stabbed her. What had this woman been to Noah? Why did she hold such power over him? Had she only been kind when no one else was during his captivity? Or had it been something more?

Kristen flung a conjured ball of purple electricity at Noah. He growled as it scorched his skin, then she turned and ran. Kristen knew as well as Sydney did that Noah couldn't bring himself to end her life. But Sydney could.

Hostility and rage surged through her. The woman had been kind enough when Sydney was captured, but the way she looked at Noah, the way he'd hesitated... Somewhere in the irrational place where the simultaneous claim and mating bond lived, Sydney couldn't let the bitch live.

She pulled a knife from a concealment band under her top and put on a burst of vampiric speed. She'd slit the woman's throat before Noah could reach them.

His eyes glowed golden. "Why did you do that? She was running."

Sydney licked the blood off the knife, then bit into Kristen's throat, draining the body before letting it drop. Killing with fangs felt too personal, but once her foe was dead, the call of her powerful magical blood had been too much to resist.

Shame washed over her. All these years she'd lived like a human with an odd diet. It was only now at her full power, confronted with jealousy and mating links and rage, that she'd let the monster out. And for the briefest moment, she'd felt that scary predatory calm and lack of remorse. She brushed past Noah to join the fight in earnest. She needed to do some killing she could more easily justify to paper over the petty murder she'd just committed. But he grabbed her arm to stop her.

"Sydney."

"Don't. I don't know what I am now. I can't believe I just..." Yeah, Tam had said to leave no survivors, and it was debatable if disobeying that order for one additional person would make a difference. But they both knew that wasn't why Kristen was a drained corpse at the edge of the woods right now.

Noah pulled Sydney into his arms, and she laid her head against his shoulder. He petted her hair as she sobbed. "You've never been tested before. You've never had to deal with the consequences of your power before because it's new."

"Have you? Had to deal with consequences?"

He was silent, and she knew that it wasn't the same for him. He hadn't been damaged by the lives he'd taken.

"She made her choice to come here to fight," he said.

"Was there something between the two of you?"

Noah's eyes widened. "Is that why you...? No. She was just nice to me. She was a friend. Or the closest thing I had in there."

If he thought that would make Sydney feel better, he was wrong. She just cried harder.

"I don't think we should fight anymore unless they need us. You're too upset." He started to lead her away, but she stubbornly refused to go with him.

The fight started to die down, but she ran headlong into it, anyway.

Her father fought and ripped heads off bodies, his face covered in blood like a madman. Was that what she was, too?

Hundreds of bodies littered the landscape. The enemy. Not the preternaturals this time.

Tam, Dayne, and Anna were starting to run out of energy. A powerfully bright ball of fire hurtled toward the group of them. Dayne didn't see it in time. Before Sydney could call out a warning, Fiona jumped in front of it.

"No!" Sydney shouted as the witch fell. Hadrian and Angeline rushed to try to heal her, but it was too late.

The black panther roared and attacked the magic user who'd thrown the fire. The two of them struggled and fought, the magic user unable to overcome Z's pure rage and grief. The demons converged on the remaining few humans and killed them quickly.

Z emerged from his fight and struggled to reclaim his human form. He was wounded but alive.

The core group stood over the fallen witch as the demons faded back into the forest, no doubt headed back to Cain's dimension.

Birds flew over Fiona, circling her, their shrill calls deafening in the forest fogged up from the smoke of too much magic.

Sydney was sure she imagined it, but it sounded like they were saying: "I told you so. I told you so."

Z let out an agonized cry when he reached her, and the animals fled back into the forest. Even the birds dispersed as he sobbed over her.

Noah gripped Sydney's hand. She knew he was thinking what if it had been her? It could have just as easily been her. Z held the witch's limp body in his arms. He was shaking from grief.

A black cat tentatively approached the circle, then Aunt Greta shifted back. For the first time she seemed unconcerned with her nudity. "It's my fault. I asked her to watch out for Dayne. I had a bad feeling. I didn't mean for her to get hurt."

Z didn't seem to hear her, or else he refused to acknowledge the apology.

"We might not have won without her," Tam said. "It was an honor to teach her her craft. She came so far from when we first met. Her animal communication gifts expanded and grew stronger. And she was much braver than she ever thought she was."

But none of these platitudes soothed the angry and distraught panther.

"What was the point? She died, anyway. If she'd left well enough alone with the magic, we could have had decades more together. I didn't care about the gray hair." He looked up at Tam, his eyes glittering gold. "Bring her back!"

"I can't, Z."

"Bring. Her. Back. It's your fault. Bring her back. If you're so fucking powerful, bring her back. Or is your reputation just so much noise? Am I supposed to be impressed by you? I'll be impressed when you can bring a motherfucking soul back from the grave. So do it!"

"I can't. I can't call her back. She's in heaven now. She can't come back to this body. It's done. I can't defy the laws of magic anymore than a normal human can defy physics."

"Then send me to her."

"You know how it is in heaven. You can't be with her there like you were with her here."

"The hell I can't. Let them try and stop us."

Sydney expected Tam to give the panther some speech about how time healed wounds, how he would recover and get better, how he needed to work through the grief. But she didn't. She simply nodded grimly and raised her arms above her head. She chanted in Latin as the energy gathered around her into a ball of brilliant light, then she sent it straight into him.

Z slumped over Fiona, and it was done.

Tam turned toward the shaking, skinny guy whose magic had been bound. "You are going back to the hub city. You get to live. You're welcome. You will tell them that we will not negotiate with them. If we see them near our borders, we will kill them. We have access to all the demons in the demon dimension. We will not be defeated any further. They will leave us alone, and we will leave them alone. They can't have everything. They can't have everyone. They most certainly can't have us. Do you understand?"

"Y-y-yes." The guy stumbled back when she released the energetic band that held him captive.

It was hard to believe he was a magic user. He seemed new, far too new to have been sent on this mission. He wasn't foolish enough to try to use his powers now, not while so outnumbered with the bodies of his associates at his feet.

"Do you think he'll make it back?" Noah asked as the lone survivor scrambled off the way they'd arrived.

"I'll send Henry to find out later."

"What about the bodies?" Sydney said. They couldn't just leave them there. Fiona and Z should be buried properly.

"I'll take care of it tomorrow after I've rested," Tam said. "We'll have a memorial service for the witch and the panther."

"Do you remember them from when you were a pup?" Sydney whispered.

"Bits and pieces," Noah said. "She made good grilled cheese." He started to lead Sydney back toward town.

Anthony approached the two of them, wiping blood off his face and trying not to look like a total sociopath while he did it. He side-hugged Sydney and kissed her on the cheek. "Come see your mother tomorrow, okay? I'm sure she'll be back to normal in a few days, but you should come by."

"Okay."

He looked over at Noah, his face going dark. "If you ever hurt her..."

"Oh my God, dad. Noah won't ever hurt me."

Anthony dragged his finger across his own throat, his eyes cold and dead as he continued to threaten her mate. "I will put your head on a pike if you do, boy." Then before either of them could respond, he disappeared into the woods.

Cole and Jane fell into step beside them. Jane looked perfect as ever. It was hard to tell if she'd been injured and had already healed, or if she was covering injuries with a demon glamour. Cole had a gash in his side that still sparked with magic but was slowly closing. It might have killed him if he wasn't fully immortal like Jane.

Cole clapped Noah on the back. "You need electrical and Internet at your place?"

"Yeah," Noah said. It was still awkward between the two of them. The time and distance would take a while to close. "And running water would be nice, but it's not necessary."

"Speak for yourself," Sydney said. "I'm not pooping in the woods."

Cole winked at her. "We can't let the princess poop in the woods."

Jane shot Sydney a look that said, *I told you he'd come around.*

It was only then that Sydney realized their pack wasn't there. And neither was Cole's.

"Where are the wolves?"

"We voted after you left with Fiona. We didn't want to risk them or anyone we couldn't protect. It's why we brought the demons in," Jane said. "We didn't want to give the humans the satisfaction of casualties."

That plan had almost worked.

Jane and Cole left them and went back toward the hive. The entire group was going off in their own directions. Sydney wondered if once the wards were up they'd ever have the bonds they'd had so many years ago before all this.

They'd won. She should feel happy, but all she felt was tired. And it was still hours until the sun would rise.

Noah tugged on her hand. "Come on, Sydney. The world just changed. We're free."

EPILOGUE

year later.

NOAH SAT at a long table on the roof of the penthouse next to his mate. The Cary Town Luxury Apartments were fully redone—almost back to their glory days from decades earlier. The pool had water. The elevators worked. And they'd managed to restore the cherry wood paneling in the lobby and hallways, much to Sydney's delight.

That had been Anthony's project. Who knew the vampire was so attached to paneling? Though perhaps it had been an excuse to spend time with his daughter to build a relationship that wasn't based on keeping her under lock and key.

Jane and Greta were conspiring near the pool—Greta

in her cat form and Jane mimicking it. They meowed at each other even though Noah was pretty sure Jane didn't speak Catonese. Dayne was on the other end of the roof speaking with Luc and Anna, unaware that Cole's mate was about to try to fool him with her shapeshifting disguise.

Anthony stood next to the grill making burgers and grumbling loudly about it.

"Make mine rare," Noah said.

The vampire king wrinkled his nose at the meat as he flipped it. Charlee brought out more meat patties, and he growled. He didn't do menial labor, and losing his former position as Master of All He Surveyed, wasn't sitting well. But there was no longer any excuse he could give for why he had to be such a control freak.

After Tam had made sure the new borders and wards were secure—with several layers of magical security redundancy—Cole had come in and added his own brand of high-tech security to the mix.

As rumors spread, therians and vampires without a home began to seek refuge again in Cary Town. Cain brought gold he'd been hoarding in a cave in his dimension to create commerce as the city began to grow and flourish again.

At Noah's suggestion, a large tree house was built in the place of a previous park, standing as a memorial to Fiona and Z.

Cary Town was not without its logistical problems in the absence of a human population. To deal with the lack of humans to feed from, therians who were given shelter in the city were required to donate their blood to a vampire.

Therians weren't thrilled, but there was so much wildlife in the Cary Town forest and so much protection in the city itself, that becoming a vampire meal seemed better than the life they'd left behind.

Tam's message had indeed been delivered by the scrawny guy, and no one from the hub city—let alone an army—dared venture near their borders. It didn't mean they never would, but for now there was peace.

It was full dark, and the whole gang was on the roof now. With the new wards and their city returning to life, they'd all come back together—for the first time feeling as if they were all on the same side. Even Hadrian, the vampire from the church, had joined them. His shy mate, Angeline, clung close to him.

The stories of the past were still told about this spat or that one, about one of them torturing or trying to kill another of them, about being on opposite teams, and about being on the same team only for expediency. They'd each been the heroes of their own stories and the villains of others. But for the first time, they were all truly united. Somehow along the way they'd found friends. They'd found family. And most importantly, they'd found love.

ABOUT THE AUTHOR

To hear about new releases first, sign up for my new release list at: www.kittythomas.com

The Complete Fated Mates Series:

Book 1: Blood Lust
    Book 2: Incubus Awakened
    Book 3: Hunted
    Book 4: Bad Magic
    Book 5: Forbidden
    Book 6: Caged Moon

Thank you for reading and supporting my work!

Kitty ^.^

ACKNOWLEDGMENTS

Cover Art: Robin Ludwig at gobookcoverdesign.com (I think this is my favorite cover design so far! I said this exact thing about the last cover, but I really mean it this time. She's gotten so good I'm going to make her redo my earlier covers. Robin, I'm just kidding, don't read this! Look over there! A puppy!)

Digital Formatting and moral support: Tom (I love you more than Starbucks.)

Editorial Assistance: Karen and Michelle. Thanks for getting it back to me so quickly. And Karen thanks also for helping brainstorm with me for the title! Without you I would have yet another title (I've got two between two pen names) that had the word "Blood" in it.